T0368105

House of Mirrors

BERNADETTE WULF

authorHOUSE®

AuthorHouse™
1663 Liberty Drive
Bloomington, IN 47403
www.authorhouse.com
Phone: 833-262-8899

© 2024 Bernadette Wulf. All rights reserved.

No part of this book may be reproduced, stored in a retrieval system, or transmitted by any means without the written permission of the author.

This is a work of fiction. All of the characters, names, incidents, organizations, and dialogue in this novel are either the products of the author's imagination or are used fictitiously.

Published by AuthorHouse 11/19/2024

ISBN: 979-8-8230-3606-1 (sc)

Print information available on the last page.

Any people depicted in stock imagery provided by Getty Images are models, and such images are being used for illustrative purposes only. Certain stock imagery © Getty Images.

Cover art by GetCovers.com
Back Cover Author Photo by Benjamin Aronoff

This book is printed on acid-free paper.

Because of the dynamic nature of the Internet, any web addresses or links contained in this book may have changed since publication and may no longer be valid. The views expressed in this work are solely those of the author and do not necessarily reflect the views of the publisher, and the publisher hereby disclaims any responsibility for them.

CHAPTER 1

Breaking Point

The house was dark and silent as Julia crept into her Uncle Ralph's bedroom, a long kitchen knife clutched in her trembling hand. She moved like a predator stalking its prey, her face flushed, heart pounding.

Time seemed to stand still as she crept closer to Ralph's bed. The air felt thick with a sense of impending doom. Julia held her breath. Her heart felt as if it would burst from her chest as she leaned over him, the knife poised above his neck ready to strike, moonlight glinting off its razor-sharp edge.

In the distance, a siren wailed. The sheer curtains billowed in a sudden gust of wind. Ralph stirred in his sleep, groaning. Julia froze, overwhelmed with emotions — confusion, dread, and a dark wrath that threatened to consume her.

Her eyes were fixed on Ralph's throat at the spot where she meant to plunge the knife and end his life, and a vision flashed before her — Ralph's lifeless pale eyes blindly staring in shock as a red tide oozed over his pillow.

Julia recoiled in horror, jolting herself awake. Her eyes flew open and she inhaled with a sudden, startled gasp. She was inexplicably next to her Uncle Ralph's bed, a knife glinting ominously in her grip. The remnants of a fierce rage still throbbed within her, fueling her bewilderment. How had she made her way to his room? And why was she holding a knife?

Tears streamed down her face as she staggered backward, the knife slipping from her grasp and landing with a soft thud on the thick pile carpet.

"What am I doing? I c-can't...," she gasped.

Julia's mind spun in a whirlwind of chaos and pain as she fled the room, her pulse pounding in her temples and her breath straining in ragged gasps. Something had snapped inside of her, a dam of emotions had burst and left her feeling raw and exposed.

It was only a nightmare, she told herself. She had been sleepwalking — but what if it happened again?

She could not go on the way things were. What if she had actually murdered her uncle? She knew she couldn't stay. Not even for another hour. Not after what she'd almost done.

This isn't who I am, she told herself. Her mind strained to remember better times, before the darkness took hold — how she had bottle-fed a litter of kittens she had found abandoned in a storm drain, volunteered at the animal shelter, and collected food for homeless children. These memories of her kindness and empathy starkly contrasted with the scene that had just unfolded, reminding her of who she really wanted to be.

Dashing to her bedroom, Julia yanked her backpack out of the closet and crammed it full of warm sweaters, cotton T-shirts, blue jeans, a hair brush, toothbrush, socks and underwear. As she strapped her sleeping bag to the backpack, she recalled her grandmother's words, "You have a heart of gold, my dear, but your temper is the redhead's curse." Julia was determined to prove her wrong. She had to regain control of her life and her emotions.

She pulled open a dresser drawer, grabbed a pile of cash hidden under her pajamas and stuffed it into her pocket. She had been saving her pet-sitting money for years, not being the type to squander it on clothes and makeup the way some of her friends did. All that stuff was superficial nonsense in her opinion.

As prepared as she could ever be for the void into which she seemed to be falling, Julia threw on a heavy jacket, shouldered her backpack and headed for the kitchen to grab a bunch of bananas, a water bottle and a bag of granola. At the front door, she hesitated as she reached for the doorknob. Once she turned that knob everything would change. She didn't know where to go or what she would do next, but, she reminded herself, anywhere else had to be better than living here with the rage that threatened to consume her soul.

A gust of chilly wind rushed in as she pulled open the door and she braced herself to face the unknown. Stepping out beneath a sky full of stars, she resolutely marched forward, feeling a mixture of dread and relief.

She glanced back only once. The house was cloaked in shadow, its dark roofline stark against the starry sky, the walls blending with the houses on either side. Like a black hole, she mused.

Julia didn't have a car, so she headed on foot toward the Greyhound bus station a few blocks away, bought a ticket and climbed aboard the first bus heading north. It was less civilized up there, she figured — better for hiding out.

She wondered what Ralph would think when he found her gone — what he would make of the knife on his bedroom floor. It almost made her chuckle sarcastically, but a wave of remorse quickly washed away her amusement. She must have subconsciously wanted to murder him, but she knew she was better than that. She had to be.

CHAPTER 2

Three Months Later

Flames surround me, licking, crackling, searing my skin like devouring monsters. The stench of smoke and my burning flesh chokes my lungs. My body recoils, yet I feel detached. There is no pain. I feel peaceful, even blissful.

I feared this was the end, but now I realize it was only the beginning.

Ralph slammed the diary shut. A digital alarm clock glowed on Julia's bedside table counting off the seconds.

He was seated on the edge of her bed, looking very much out of place on her pink-flowered bedspread with his neatly trimmed fringe of red-gray hair and bald scalp. In the harsh light of Julia's reading lamp, Ralph looked tired and old beyond his years. He hadn't been sleeping well and it showed in the sunken shadows under his eyes.

With an irritated sigh, he glared at the diary as if it was the source of his distress. His hands shook slightly and his breathing felt constricted. Why couldn't he read Julia's diary without feeling so guilty?

The girl, his only niece, had vanished three months ago. Her diary might be the only clue to her whereabouts. Still, as he examined the worn volume in his hands, he felt a sense of outrage imploding in his gut. His fists tightened. His temples throbbed.

"Damn!" He grumbled. "What's the matter with me?"

The diary, a fresh reminder of Julia's disappearance, triggered his all-too-familiar feeling of panic. He felt out of control. The image of the gleaming butcher knife on his bedroom carpet flashed in his mind. He glanced behind him — a nervous habit he had developed in childhood.

Resolutely, Ralph forced himself to open the diary again and squinted to focus on the inside front cover. Julia's writing was usually delicate and easy to read, but here the angles were sharp and the pen strokes heavy, as though she had been forcing the words onto the page in anger or haste. The entry was dated July thirteenth. Ralph felt a shiver run up his spine. That was the day before she disappeared.

> *I dedicate this diary to Tom, because he was such a compassionate executioner. Now we weave another web. I wonder what karma has in store for us this time?*

"Executioner? Karma? What the hell?" Ralph scratched his head with a frown.

Did Julia have a premonition, even three months ago, about Tom's recent tragedy? She had a history of premonitions. But why would she add this dedication to the beginning of her diary after she had been writing in it for months? Eight-and-a-half months judging from the dated entries.

Tom, her best friend since they were toddlers, had given her the diary at her last birthday party, Halloween night. That was almost a year ago. Her first entry was dated the following day. All Saints Day, Ralph noted to himself with a cynical snort. He doubted there were any saints involved in this story.

Details of Julia's party flashed back clearly as Ralph pondered what he had just read. He could still picture his niece dancing across the living room in her witch costume with the long black cape and a big pointed hat perched atop her flowing auburn hair. Her tresses were like wildfire streaming down her back and over her shoulders, sometimes lashing across her face. Her eyes glowed like amber in a face full of freckles.

It was her eighteenth birthday party. Her coming of age. A celebration of her emancipation. Yet Julia had always seemed very independent to Ralph. She had taken care of herself quite well, even as a child.

Nonetheless, this birthday was a milestone for him. Up until then, he had been her legal guardian. Now she was free to do whatever she pleased — and he had a feeling she wasn't interested in pleasing him at all. At this point, though she made his blood boil, he just hoped that she was alive and safe.

It didn't help that people in his local parish at Ascension Catholic church seemed to be wondering what he had done to drive her away. Not that they said anything. He could just tell from the way they looked at him. Like it had to be his fault.

Ralph had done his best to care for Julia since she was thirteen, mostly because he couldn't stomach the idea of letting his mother ruin another child. She, Carol McCullen, had tried to get custody of Julia, but Ralph fought her tooth and nail. In his opinion both he and his sister had fared badly at the hands of their mother. Not that their mother was an evil person. Certainly not. She was widely admired as the epitome of decency and virtue.

Her home always shone with cleanliness and normalcy, as did her personal appearance. Indeed, she was the very image of social grace and culture. Everything she did fit perfectly within the expectations of her staunch, middle-class Irish Catholic peers. A better model mother could not be found. Yet somehow her two children had grown up to be terrible misfits.

Ralph's sister, Missy, was gone now, leaving a void in Ralph's life. Nobody else could understand what life had been like in their childhood home. Missy and her husband had been killed in a private plane crash when Julia was thirteen.

It still baffled Ralph, the way Julia had sensed it before it happened. She had warned her parents not to go, even begged them. Everyone thought she was being melodramatic, a typical teenager thinking only of herself. It was a very awkward situation for Ralph as her babysitter. A thirteen-year-old can be quite a handful, even if it is only melodrama.

Sadly, it turned out that Julia was right. She had spent the whole day crying. By the time everyone else got the news, her tears were spent. With a weary shrug, she went on with her life. A melancholy smile was her only outward sign of grief. That had troubled Ralph.

An air of resigned complacency hung over Julia, as if something inside of her had died. Feelings that were too strong to bear seemed to have been walled off. Still, she did well at school and seemed comfortable with her classmates. She laughed loud and often. Too loud sometimes. Ralph could still picture her mingling with the guests at her birthday party, entertaining them with her wry sense of humor.

It was obvious then that Tom doted on her. He blushed whenever she teased him, and especially when he handed her his birthday gift, the diary Ralph now held in his hands.

Ralph looked down at the little book, remembering the intimate glance that had passed between Julia and Tom when she first leafed through its empty pages. Such a curious smile had played about her lips.

"I hope I get to read it someday," Tom had quipped, a quick grin flashing across his handsome face. It was Julia's turn to blush.

CHAPTER 3

Disappearing Act

After Julia fled her uncle's bedroom that fateful night, she felt a steely determination to get as far away from Ralph as possible, no matter what.

On boarding her bus, she took the wide seat at the far back and stretched out on her side, hoping she could claim the whole seat for herself. Focusing on her breath, she tried to calm herself and slow the pounding of her heart. She could still feel the sensation of the knife handle pressed against her palm.

Though she had left it on the floor of Ralph's bedroom, the image of the knife blade gleaming in the moonlight was etched in her mind. She shuddered, imagining Ralph's face as he discovered the knife on the floor next to his bed. A wave of guilt washed over her and her eyes filled with tears.

It didn't occur to Julia to be afraid. She was still jacked up on adrenalin and rage. Worn down by months of horrifying nightmares and sleepless nights, all she wanted now was peace — escape from the relentless memories that haunted her.

As the bus pulled out of the station, she sat up and blinked back her tears, watching as her old life passed slowly into the night. Familiar city streets melted into shadowy suburban neighborhoods until dawn revealed a wide open countryside, rolling golden hills and farmlands stretching out for miles in every direction. In the distance, jagged peaks of the Sierra Nevada mountains were silhouetted by the first rays of sunshine.

Julia supposed she would intuitively know when she arrived at the best place to get off the bus — somewhere with trees and water and wilderness, far from human civilization. Meanwhile, she thought about her past and tried to understand how she had made such a mess of her life. Her anger had now subsided into confusion, pain and a feeling of hopelessness.

She strained to remember good times before the haunting memories of burning and betrayal had eclipsed everything else. Not that she had ever been really happy since her parents died, but at least she had been able to have fun.

In high school she had been the life of the party in her little group of friends, always the one to come up with plans for movie nights, camping trips, themed potlucks and the like, but the girls had slowly distanced themselves as Julia became more and more irritable and angry. Only Tom remained. Her faithful friend.

Now she wouldn't even be close to Tom. She was totally alone on a Greyhound bus bound for what felt like an endless void.

CHAPTER 4

The Diary

Ralph ran his fingers over the embossed cover of Julia's diary, wondering why he had only discovered it three months after she vanished. He had found it tucked under her mattress when he was changing her sheets for a visiting cousin. The way its key had dropped to the floor at his feet made it seem as if Julia had planned it that way. But why would she? Perhaps further reading would answer his question. He snorted at the irony. So far it was only bringing up more questions.

Ralph took the diary to the living room and settled back against the overstuffed cushions of his couch. He opened to the first page, skimming over descriptions of Julia's birthday party. After flipping through several pages, a different slant of her handwriting caught his eye. Her whole tone had changed. He started to read in earnest, a puzzled frown furrowing his brow.

> *I'm beginning to remember things that frighten me. Things I can't explain, but they're so real I can't deny them either. This morning I saw myself tied to a post and engulfed in flames. Tom was there watching. There were tears in his eyes, but he never moved to rescue me. He couldn't. He was the executioner. His job was to start the fire. His personal feelings had to be set aside.*

I could feel heat searing my flesh as the flames lashed at my legs. I struggled, screamed, and then gave up, surrendering to the pain. Then suddenly it was all turned inside out. The pain became pleasure. The pleasure overflowed into ecstasy. And as I watched Tom standing there beside the bonfire, I knew he could never understand.

I was outside my body, watching scarlet flames lick at my charred skin, black smoke billowing out, rising up in acrid waves. My eyes were glazed over in anguish. Black eyes. So different from the color they are now.

Tom (or whatever his name was then) went stiff, his eyes wide. I know he wanted to save me. He couldn't know that I was by his side watching. I was free of pain. I guess I was already dead, but he was fixated on my body. It was still writhing.

Then the vision was over. I couldn't remember anything more, but I knew it was real. It wasn't just a dream. I was wide awake. It was so mesmerizing to watch my body being consumed by flames. No wonder I have always been fascinated by fire, and by the idea of death. What is death if I could be there watching?

And now, as I look back, it all seems connected, all my years of nightmares, my visions of fire, hearing screams in the night — and Tom. He is so attentive to me. He worries about me. I don't think he remembers burning me, but now he chooses to spend time with me over all the other girls who want him, even though I'm not as pretty or as popular.

He looked so different in that lifetime. His eyes were dark like mine were, and he was short and stocky. I couldn't see his face with the black hood over his head, but I had a sense that he was Spanish or Moorish. Maybe I was too. I had the same dark hair and eyes.

Just now I went to look in the mirror to see if there was any similarity in my looks. All I could see was the fire, flickering in my eyes and glowing in my hair as though my dark coloring had been burned away and only the flames remained. No wonder Tom is drawn to me. Something in him must remember. He just doesn't know what it is... yet.

Ralph dropped the diary on his lap, beads of perspiration gathering on his forehead. Could it have been a dream she was remembering, or was she raving mad? Madness seemed to run in the family, after all. Julia's mother had even spent a couple of months in a mental institution.

Then another thought sent a chill into Ralph's bones. What if Julia had truly been executed in some former life by this boy who was now her best friend? And if so, what was her crime?

He set the diary on the coffee table, planning to read more when he had a chance. It was almost a year ago that Julia had first written about the burning. She wrote that she had been having horrible nightmares for months, but she had never mentioned any of it to Ralph. He wished that she could have trusted him more than that.

Soon it would be her birthday again. There was a crisp chill in the October air and he had seen gold and scarlet leaves dancing on the wind that morning. Ralph wondered if Julia would even be alive to see her nineteenth birthday.

He slammed his fist on the arm of the couch as a surge of frustration shot through him. She was so exasperating! She made him feel guilty and that made him angry. But why should he feel guilty when she was the one who had abandoned him in the night, leaving no explanation but a knife on his bedroom floor.

He jolted at the thought of it. Had she meant to kill him? Was it a cryptic message? He could feel his blood pressure rising as he struggled to understand.

Ralph was supposed to be her guardian, but what did she care? After all the years she had lived with him, her sudden disappearance felt like a sharp slap in the face. He knew that if she'd been abducted, she wouldn't have been able to take her backpack and sleeping bag. It was obviously her choice to leave and that galled him.

He thought back to all the times he and Julia had butted heads: the battles over her refusal to go to church, the many times he had grounded her for staying out past her curfew, her resistance to his demands that she help with cleaning and cooking — typical teenage stuff. But had it really been so bad?

There was the guilt again. He knew he could have been so much better, kinder, more understanding. He could have supported her, rather than trying to control her, but he had been so preoccupied with his own demons that he barely noticed hers.

It wasn't that he didn't love her, he told himself. He did, in his own muddled way. He really wanted the best for her, but he hadn't been able to express it to her very well. If he had, maybe she wouldn't have run away.

Of course he had filed a missing person's report with the police, but after three months of investigations and wide-ranging searches they still hadn't found a trace of her. She had left her cell phone behind and had no credit cards to trace.

And even though the surveillance cameras at the bus station had captured footage of a woman buying a ticket early that morning, she had been hidden beneath a floppy hat, sunglasses, and a scarf covering her mouth and nose, as if intentionally trying to hide her identity. Unfortunately, bus stations were not like airports where she would have had to identify herself. Maybe she was gone for good.

CHAPTER 5

Another World

The date was July fourteenth in a year that felt like the end of time. Julia had stepped off the Greyhound bus at an isolated stop surrounded by thick forest with a beautiful stream running through it. She had been looking forward to this year with eager anticipation, her year of emancipation. Finally, she had turned eighteen. Now that she was an adult she had the power to make her own decisions and run her own life. But what was left of that life? Nothing!

The year had started off well enough. She still had girlfriends back when she turned eighteen. The nightmares were less frequent then and not so disturbing. She had graduated from high school with honors and made a plan to attend the local Community College. Once she had her general education requirements out of the way, she hoped to get into veterinary school so she could devote her life to helping animals.

Her plan made sense until the horrid memories began to overtake her life. They grew in intensity, starting out as nightmares and evolving into waking hallucinations that consumed her life. Now, as she stood by the bus in the middle of nowhere, she could think of nothing but the flames — and the knife she had held at her uncle's throat.

For a moment, she stood watching the bus as it vanished around a bend in the road. Then she resolutely turned, took a deep breath and trudged into the forest. She wandered aimlessly, kicking rocks and dry branches in her path, knowing it was impossible to go home after last night. Memories rose up in her consciousness like fish gasping for breath at the surface of a stagnant pool. None of them were pleasant. Her skin crawled at the thought of facing Uncle Ralph again, now that she knew what he had done to her in the past.

Her spirit felt shattered. It didn't matter where she walked. Her feet led the way. When at last she dropped to the ground, exhausted, she had no idea where she was. It wasn't important. One place felt as desolate as another.

That is when she received the gift of the black widow spider — red and black, fire and smoke, blood and charred flesh, ripe lips reflected in black eyes — her lips in his eyes. The leering eyes of the Inquisitor engulfed her, brazenly exploring her naked body as she stood shivering before him, shaven from head to toe, with her abusive husband standing by, egging him on. Reality spun.

"Admit that you consorted with the devil, witch!" The Inquisitor hissed the words. Relentlessly, he prodded her with the tip of his knife, leaving tiny drops of blood on her skin. "You may be saved from hellfire if you repent of your sins, but refusal to answer will only prove your guilt."

She felt like spitting in his face, but her mouth was parched. Biting her lip, she turned her head away, shivering. Her flesh crawled with goose bumps and her hands felt numb from the cold. The Inquisitor's eyes devoured her, seething with lust and disdain. To him, a woman was the embodiment of sin and he prided himself on being able to walk so near to temptation without succumbing. His was the power to destroy her, and in so doing he believed he could rid the world of one more occasion of sin.

Striding around her in his Dominican's black-hooded cowl, this self-proclaimed man of God accused her of every hideous crime his twisted mind could imagine. Julia watched it all in horror. Inside of her this helpless, dark-eyed woman lived, breathed and suffered, but Julia could do nothing to release her. This was the pain she was born with.

In all Julia's years at Catholic school, no nun or priest had ever mentioned the Inquisition. Nobody had tried to explain why the church had persisted in torturing and killing women who practiced midwifery or healing, or widows who lived alone, particularly if they were wealthy. No one had mentioned how thousands of Jews, Romanies and homosexuals had been rounded up, tortured and burned by a church that preached a doctrine of love.

Such a huge segment of European history seemed oddly forgotten. But Julia remembered. All through her childhood she had dreamed of the burning times. Those dreams haunted her even more relentlessly now that she had uncovered Ralph's former identity. With startling clarity, the horrors of her distant past engulfed her present, until she could think of nothing else.

Delirious, Julia pulled herself to her feet. She felt feverish. The spider bite on her ankle had swollen to a huge red lump and the lymph glands in her groin ached and throbbed. In spite of the swelling and pain, she was able to stumble along as if in a dream. The spider's poison seemed to have worked its way to her brain. She thought it might kill her, but it hardly mattered. All she knew, somewhere in the back of her mind, was that she had to keep moving in the same direction. That was her only hope.

Shuffling forward, she dragged her swollen foot as if it was made of wood. A chill crept in upon her, sinking into blood and bone, numbing her senses. She welcomed the numbness. Her nerves were so raw that she simply didn't want to feel anymore.

When at last Julia came to a path wide enough to lie down on, she collapsed, letting her body nestle along its length close to the cool hard Earth. Her flaming hair was the only sign of life, lifting in the breeze and tangling in the bushes that shaded her from the intense summer sun. She lay almost motionless, sweating and shivering as the warm afternoon breezes blew over her. In time she would feel nothing at all.

CHAPTER 6

Margaret Littlewolf

Margaret Littlewolf had spent the day collecting wild herbs and berries as she meandered through the wooded area just west of her rustic hut. It was her habit to wander by herself and explore the countryside. She was old now, and she reckoned it was her right to do whatever she pleased. Old people could. All her life she had been there for others. Now she wanted time for herself.

Margaret was aware, though, that her knowledge of healing was valuable and she didn't mind sharing it. All her experience as a medicine woman and midwife had made her indispensable to her tribe, and to many of the country folk in the area. There weren't any doctors out here. Besides, most of the backwoods people didn't trust doctors. They trusted her.

Many local children owed their lives to Margaret. She had delivered them into the world, nursed them through fevers, splinted their broken bones and told them stories about the days when her people wove baskets beside the river.

It was important to her that the wisdom of her people lived on, even if only in the hearts of white folks. As she grew older, she came to see herself more as a storyteller than a healer. But in a sense, she thought to herself, telling stories was the best way to heal.

This afternoon she was inspired by the brilliance of the July sun flashing through the leafy canopy overhead. Every season seemed precious to her now. She felt a finality in these long days, knowing this might well be the last summer she would ever see. Margaret wanted to live it fully and deeply, weaving her long and rich experience of life into the fabric of the present moment.

In the crisp cool dawn she had filled her backpack with enough food and water to last the day, wrapped herself warmly and headed out to the wonders of nature. Something tugged at her heart as she walked beneath the arching branches of the white oaks and bay trees. They were so peaceful and yet so vital. These trees would be standing long after she was gone. That gave her comfort.

Stealthily, she crept along a creek bank trying not to make a sound. In her youth she had been able to sneak up on wildlife so silently that they never knew she was there. Now she was not so light on her feet. Her old legs moved slowly and heavily and her sandals were worn from shuffling over rocks, but she loved to walk. It didn't matter where. Every direction was interesting.

As Margaret neared a familiar path, a strange movement caught her eye. It looked as if a long wisp of red hair was caught in a tangle of branches, blowing in the summer breeze. She moved closer. There, almost hidden in the overgrowth, was a human body. She bent down cautiously and began to brush away sticks and leaves from the face. Her apprehension began to lift as she felt warm breath on her hands. The girl was unconscious, but alive.

It took all Margaret's strength to lift the limp body and prop it against her. She rubbed the clammy fingers and patted the cheeks until at last the eyelids fluttered open.

"Poor thing," she muttered. "You could have died out here."

"Uh," the girl groaned. "I want to die."

"Don't say such a thing, child. You can't mean it," the old woman fixed her with a stern gaze. "Why don't you tell me your name? I'll do what I can to help you."

"Julia. Julia Flynn," the girl whispered through parched lips.

"Well, Julia, we don't have time to waste. That bite on your ankle needs attention. Let's see if you can walk with me. I'll take you somewhere more comfortable."

With that the old woman fell silent and concentrated all her energy on getting Julia to stand and walk. About half a mile away there was a small hut that Margaret stayed in from time to time. It was damp and shaded, but it would be cozy once she made a fire. Twilight had overtaken the sun by the time the two women stumbled through the doorway into the hut, each feeling too exhausted to take another step. Margaret helped Julia onto a cot against the wall and sat herself down on a rough wooden chair at the bedside.

"I'm gettin' too old for this," she groaned to herself, leaning back in her chair with a weary sigh. But in another moment she was up, piling kindling on the fireplace grate and arranging it in a perfect little teepee. One strike of a match and the room glowed with cheery light.

"I'm sorry," Julia's voice murmured through a daze. "I don't want to put you to any trouble."

"Never you mind, Julia. It's my pleasure to help somebody in need." Margaret was crouched in front of the fire and she stood up with great effort, looking toward Julia. "Now, I want you to rest there while I mix you up some medicine. You've got a nasty black widow bite on that leg of yours, but we'll soon take care of that."

Margaret poked a long stick into the fire and knocked a chunk of charcoal onto the hearth. After letting it cool for a moment, she crushed it into a powder and mixed it with witch hazel tincture from a bottle she kept on a shelf by the door. She applied a thick layer of the resulting paste to Julia's spider bite. Margaret then wrapped it with a cloth bandage, explaining that it would draw out the toxins.

Next she set to work making a strong tea of echinacea, nettle leaves and garlic, all of which were hanging in bunches along the walls of her hut.

"You feelin' warmer yet?" Margaret asked as she handed Julia a cup of the steaming tea.

"Not really," Julia answered with a shiver. "I guess I got pretty chilled."

"You have quite a fever. Your body's tryin' to fight off the spider toxin. I don't think ya would have died from the spider bite. You're a strong girl, but... a person can die from just givin' up."

The next morning Julia was strong enough to go out with Margaret for a short walk. Margaret had awakened her several times in the night and made her drink the warm, earthy tea. Julia thought it tasted awful, but it made her feel much better.

As Julia gazed up at the tall firs and pine trees surrounding her, the life she had left behind seemed to fade away, as if it had been a dream. Was it only yesterday that her pre-dawn bus ride had taken her past her old school, the library and the church rectory where her grandmother did housekeeping for the parish priest? It seemed so long ago.

Julia had an odd feeling that she had known Margaret for ages. The old woman felt so familiar and it seemed like she knew everything — the plants, the animals, the meaning of clouds moving across the sky. And Julia knew nothing. Yesterday she had been ready to die, but here was a whole new world to explore, a fascinating reality she had never even imagined.

Margaret seemed completely at home in this realm of nature. She knew how to survive, how to find food, water and herbs for healing. Julia watched as her hostess moved between the trees as deftly as she and her friends had moved through a shopping mall. And it was just like she was shopping. Julia grinned at the thought. A sprig of mistletoe from this isle, a plump mushroom from the next, a handful of berries — the basket on Margaret's arm was quickly filling.

Sometimes she found a pretty thing, like a bright blue feather. Then it would be something useful, perhaps a nice piece of firewood. With this odd assortment of collectibles, Margaret seemed quite pleased. She flashed a wrinkled smile at Julia and motioned toward the hut.

"You must be gettin' hungry. Shall we have some lunch?" Margaret's brown eyes twinkled. "I've found just the mushrooms I was lookin' for. Don't usually find 'em at this time of year, but we had a summer rain."

"I'm famished," Julia gushed. "I think I could eat anything!"

As time passed, Julia found it hard to remember whether it had been weeks or only days since she had found her way into the world of Margaret Littlewolf. The hours seemed to drift erratically. When it was daylight she followed Margaret through the woods, learning to recognize the ferns and madrones, the tracks of deer and raccoons and the distant calls of foxes and ravens. At dusk they shared meals unlike any she had ever tasted, earthy and simple, but full of flavor.

One morning Julia went out alone into the stillness of the dawn. It was getting warm already and all the forest creatures seemed to have vanished into their cool burrows and shady glens to rest through the heat of the day. She smiled at the sound of a frog in the nearby creek. Julia found herself smiling often now. Even the sight of her favorite trees brought an involuntary grin to her face. She couldn't remember ever being happier or more at peace.

The inner turmoil that had driven Julia to the woods was slowly subsiding with the passing of days. Nightmares tormented her less and less. The flames no longer seemed so close, and the eyes of the Inquisitor ceased to haunt her. Still, there were memories she couldn't shake. Memories of pain and betrayal. They still made her angry. So angry that she dared not go back to the life she had known. Not yet anyway.

"What do ya really want, Julia?" Margaret asked one evening as they sat by the fire. "I haven't wanted to pry, but I think there must be somethin' you're lookin' for out here?"

Julia looked up abruptly, a quizzical expression on her face. "I hadn't really thought about wanting anything," she answered. "I just wanted to get away from something."

"Must have been somethin' pretty terrible. Were ya bein' abused?"

"No, not really." Julia shrugged. "But I remembered being abused in another lifetime. I remembered it so clearly that I felt like it was happening now. It was consuming me."

"So ya thought ya could run away from yer own memories?"

"I don't know." Julia looked at Margaret with a pained expression and whispered, "I almost killed someone. I didn't trust myself. That makes me a horrible person, doesn't it?"

"Does it? Are ya still that person, Julia?"

"I don't think so. I don't feel like the same person at all now, but I don't know how I'd feel if I was back home with him."

"Well, do you still want ta kill him?"

"No." Julia shook her head. "I mean, I never really wanted to kill him. I was sleepwalking. It wasn't a conscious choice — and now I'm not feeling so angry anymore. I guess I just wanted to stop the horrible memories."

"Well that's a good thing." Margaret smiled. "If ya don't really want ta kill him, then yer not so bad. Right?"

"Yeah, I guess." Julia shrugged.

"We all get angry sometimes, Julia, and it's yer choice what kind of person ya wanna be. It can change every instant. Sure, yer a passionate person. Ya probably always will be, but that's good. Ya feel things deeply and ya need a way ta express yerself — just not by killin' someone."

"Yeah," Julia chuckled. "I'm really glad I woke up when I did. I don't think being a murderer would have improved my life at all."

"So what would improve yer life? If ya could change anythin' you want, what would ya change?"

"I'd make the memories go away. The bad ones, anyway. I'd stop the nightmares and the hallucinations."

"And how would that feel?"

Julia closed her eyes and took a deep breath. "Peaceful. It would feel peaceful," she sighed.

"So ya came here lookin' fer peace?"

"Yeah, I guess that's it. Peace."

Margaret patted Julia's hand. "And did ya find it?"

"I think I am starting to find it sometimes. At least I know what it feels like now."

That night in the quiet darkness, Julia thought about their conversation and let the feeling of peace envelop her. "At least I know what it feels like now," she repeated to herself in a whisper.

Julia watched three full moons come and go during her stay with Margaret Littlewolf. The passing of time didn't matter. Let the months go by as they would. She was finally feeling content and had no desire to go back to the turmoil of her former life.

Yet such contentment rarely lasts. One morning Julia awoke to find Margaret packing her belongings into the canvas backpack she always carried on her walks.

"Are you going somewhere?" Julia asked hesitantly, a lump forming in her throat.

"Been here long enough, I reckon." Margaret turned a kind face toward her. Then she went back to packing. "You can stay as long as ya want. I've taught ya what I know about how ta survive out here, but we may get snow in a few weeks and it won't be so easy then." Margaret fixed her eyes on Julia, "You might wanna think about goin' back home yerself."

The very thought sent a bolt of fear through the girl. "You don't think I could make it through the winter here?"

Margaret chuckled. "You could make it, sure, but what's the point? How long ya gonna hide from yer life?"

"But this is my life now." Julia tried to sound convincing. "That other life just gave me grief." At the same time she realized how lonely it would be without Margaret to keep her company.

"It's yer choice, Julia. All's I know is I have to leave. I'm needed somewhere else. I heard the messenger last night."

"Messenger?" Julia eyed her quizzically. "You mean that screech owl that scared the crap out of me in the middle of the night?"

"Yup," Margaret answered with an amused twinkle in her eyes. "Barn owl. A screech owl don't screech like that."

"Then why do they call it a screech owl?"

"Don' know. They jus' do." Margaret reached out her gnarled hands and took Julia's tender hands in hers. "I'll come visit you," she smiled warmly. "Maybe the winter 'll be good for ya here."

"But where will you go?" Julia protested. Echoes of the abandonment she felt at her mother's death reverberated inside of her.

"I won't be far. I'll be stayin' with my daughter. She's about five miles away at the edge of the reservation. But Julia," Margaret had an intense look in her eyes, "don't come lookin' fer me. This is yer time to get to know yerself. I'll just be a distraction now. Ya need to decide what ya really want for yerself. And remember, clear intentions pave the way. Try ta get as clear as ya can 'bout where ya want to go from here an' you'll get there."

"But I don't *know* where I want to go," Julia moaned.

"Well, what excites ya when you think about it? What feels fun or uplifting?"

"Hmm... I like taking care of animals. I like helping people. I have fun exploring nature. I don't know... maybe I could be a veterinarian. That's what I was planning before my meltdown. I like that idea."

"If that's the most excitin' thing, then go for it. That's your spirit telling ya it's yer best direction forward in life... at least for right now. Maybe it will change, but then there will be something more excitin' callin' ya." Margaret paused reflectively, "You ever heard of Joseph Campbell? He may have said the most helpful words ever spoken, 'Follow your bliss.'"

"Huh, that seems kind of the opposite of what most people do."

"And most people don't seem too happy, do they?"

"No, I guess not," Julia chuckled. "Is that what you do? Follow your bliss?"

"Darn right. I wouldn't have it any other way." With a squeeze of her fingers on Julia's wrist, Margaret turned and walked out the hut door. In a few moments she had melted into the deep shadows of the forest morning.

CHAPTER 7

Uncle Ralph

Ralph McCullen gazed at his reflection in the bathroom mirror. He worked hard to preserve an image of respectability in his local community, dressing conservatively and keeping what was left of his gray-peppered, orangutan-colored hair cropped short. Though he knew people considered him strange, he often gloated over the fact that they had no idea how strange he actually was.

He poured a third shot of vodka into his glass from the bottle he always kept on the back of the toilet — a nightly ritual which accounted for his bulbous red nose and the prominent spider veins on his cheeks. He told himself it helped him get to sleep. True enough.

Next he turned his attention to a ten gallon terrarium he had set up on a small table next to the bathroom sink. Slime trails laced the glass sides. He opened the lid and filled the small feeding dish with cornmeal and a few small leaves of lettuce, then watched as Dale and Lou, his pet garden snails, munched on the lettuce leaves. He had chosen names that could be masculine or feminine, since snails are hermaphrodites.

Ralph had an obsession with mollusks in general, garden snails in particular. The multitude of snails he kept in a larger tank outside supplied him with home-grown escargot, but he was also secretly fascinated with their hermaphroditic mating habits and the calcified "love darts" with which they stabbed each other during courtship.

He snapped the terrarium lid back on and returned his attention to the mirror, rubbing his fingers across the graying reddish stubble on his chin. Time to shave again, but it could wait until morning. Who would care anyway? In that moment he clearly felt his aloneness. It choked him with anxiety and made it hard to take a full breath.

Ralph's deepest secret was this gnawing loneliness. He tried to hide it even from himself, burying it beneath a voyeuristic preoccupation with women — and snails. Unable to form a romantic connection with a real woman, he spent untold hours scrolling through online porn sites. That was the closest he ever got to a romantic relationship, though he flirted to no avail with nearly every woman he met.

Actually, he reflected, running his fingers mindlessly over his balding scalp, those porn sites did consume an inappropriate amount of his time. He admitted that to himself whenever he prepared for his weekly confession, but he wasn't particularly ashamed. Weren't all men drawn to the mysteries women hid beneath their clothing? Even so, he made a point of keeping such activities well hidden from others. Above all, he wanted to be seen as normal and respectable, even if he knew how far from it he really was.

His sister, Missy, had been quite a different sort. She made no pretense of being normal. Didn't even seem to know the meaning of the word. She liked to wear oversized floppy hats and colorful hand-painted jeans and would sometimes burst into song in crowded places.

All during her youth she had been guided by voices. Often they gave her very useful information like telling her who was calling when the phone rang, or what people were really thinking when they said nice things to her.

Ralph suspected that Missy saw and heard many things that she never spoke about for fear of punishment. In their mother's house children could only speak of things that fit within a narrow definition of acceptability. Otherwise they would be accused of lying or vulgarity, and that usually meant being sent to their rooms with no dinner.

As she neared adolescence, Missy stopped sharing her psychic revelations, even with Ralph, and never spoke of the voices again. It seemed that she had been cured of her premonitions, but she had only bottled them up. At sixteen she suffered a breakdown and was hospitalized for two months. She returned home with a fresh and wild urge for freedom and self-expression. It wasn't long before she discovered a wide and wonderful world beyond her mother's reach. At eighteen, she ran off and got married. Six months later Julia was born.

Missy's husband, Stephen, had been a thorn in Ralph's side. A psychiatrist! The guy was a lot older than Missy and he had plenty of money. Once he had quipped that Ralph was anal-retentive, which peeved Ralph to no end. And he had diagnosed Missy as schizophrenic, but even Ralph had guessed that. As long as she stayed on her medications, she seemed fine.

Stephen was good to Missy. In her short life she had traveled the world, rubbed shoulders with the rich and famous and had a free shrink whenever things got her down. Unfortunately, it all ended when Julia was thirteen, the day Missy and Stephen died in the plane crash.

Ralph sighed as he thought of his sister and how devastated she would have been if she was still alive when her daughter disappeared. But then, Julia probably never would have run away if her mother was alive.

"It must have been me she was running from," Ralph mused aloud, "but why?" He stared at his face in the mirror. "What did I do to drive her away?"

In that moment he realized how much he missed Julia and how, even in her most rebellious moments, she had provided him with companionship and a strange sort of kinship, strained as it was. Conflicting feelings of love and fear, and a deep frustration enveloped him. Julia was an enigma, but she was his enigma — even if she didn't think he was worth her attention.

He had to get back to reading her diary. Maybe that would make sense of their relationship.

CHAPTER 8

Tom

Autumn bit fiercely into the warmth of Indian summer, shaking the last golden leaves to the ground. Tom Clark watched a doe a little way off, nibbling at the brambles beside a dry streambed. The grass along its banks was brown and shriveled after so many long, hot days. The deer were hungry.

Even the squirrels and birds, which had once filled the air with their chatter, were now strangely silent. Only the haunting whistle of a red-winged blackbird broke the silence.

Tom was waiting for Julia, his eyes scanning the edge of the woods, his heart anxious. Beautiful Julia. Before he had loved her, he would never have called her beautiful. But he had come to equate the odd turned-down corners of her smile and the amber glow of her eyes with beauty, through long familiarity and a growing attraction.

Once, he had imagined that beauty caused attraction, but now it seemed the other way around. What he was attracted to became his image of beauty, and forever after that certain shape of mouth would appear beautiful to him. That tilted nose with freckles across it. Those glowing eyes with their rusty lashes. Julia had become his ideal.

It frightened Tom, the way Julia had disappeared so suddenly three months ago, but he knew he couldn't have stopped her. He was glad, at least, that he knew where she was and that she was safe. A few days after she vanished, he had received a map in the mail showing their meeting place along with a time when she would be there waiting there for him. It included a note begging him to bring food — and asking him to keep it secret. Strange.

A thin cloud passed over the sun, diffusing the light. Overhead, two ravens circled, stark against the pale sky. Tom shivered in his down jacket, frowning. It wasn't so hard to live out here, Julia had told him. Native Americans had done it for ages. It seemed like such a harsh environment to Tom. He didn't even like to think of Julia walking through the woods alone, but she insisted. She had never allowed him to visit the hut where she was living, like she didn't trust him to keep it secret.

Tom felt a wave of protective instinct mixed with frustration at his failed attempts to influence her. He really wished he could talk her into going back home. Sometimes in the night he would wake up thinking he had heard her scream. He had an unsettling sense that she was burning, but he couldn't remember why. Cold sweat soaked his sheets. It was nothing real, he figured, but it always made him want to help her more than ever.

When Tom first visited Julia in the forest, she had told him how Margaret Littlewolf had rescued her. How she had nursed her back to health and offered her a place to live. Julia claimed that she was learning so much that she couldn't possibly leave yet. Tom guessed that anything she learned in the woods wouldn't do her much good once she got back to civilization, but Julia said her time with Margaret was more valuable than anything she had left behind in her old life.

As Tom scanned the edge of the woods, he wondered if maybe Julia had forgotten about their meeting this time. But it wasn't likely. She never forgot. And even if she did, she would have sensed that he was there waiting for her. She always seemed to know things like that somehow.

Julia was watching Tom from behind a tall oak tree. She could see the worry in his face, his fear that she might not show up. It made her smile to feel Tom's thoughts whirling around her like butterflies — tender, care-worn thoughts. He had a basket of fruit under his arm and a wool blanket.

Tom always brought such considerate gifts when he came to visit

— fresh vegetables, cans of soup and beans, bread, cookies, fruit and the like. He wanted to make sure she had everything she needed.

Even so, there were days when Julia felt like she could never have everything she needed. She thought it would be impossible to face the outside world again, but she had not told Tom that. He would have worried even more.

Through necessity, she was learning how to live in the moment, even if it was a moment of being tormented by the past. Somehow, just allowing her horrible memories to exist in the safety of the little hut in the woods made them seem less threatening.

In this moment, as she gazed at Tom, life felt perfect. It was one of those rare times when she felt like there was nothing more she could possibly want. The sounds and smells of nature acted as a healing balm to the burning in her soul. Tom's gentleness and concern soothed her aching heart. Gratitude enveloped her. There was hope.

She began hiking up the hill toward him, quiet as a deer. It was easy to surprise him by appearing quite close and making the sound of some animal or bird — a squirrel this time. He turned abruptly, as if amazed to find her there. Then relief flooded his face and he ran to embrace her.

Giggling with delight she pounced on him, wrapping her arms around his neck and kissing his cold cheek.

"Julia," he gasped with a disarming grin. "I was beginning to worry that you wouldn't come this time."

"You worry too much. I'm fine." Her eyes smiled into his as she snuggled into his arms and sighed. It was good to see him — Tom, her ever-faithful friend. Not yet a man, but no longer a boy. Standing on a hilltop, full of longing. Shivering in her arms.

It felt to Julia that he had been standing there for hundreds of years, watching for her in the glow of a bonfire.

CHAPTER 9

Lord Blackney

T he night after his cousin left, Ralph picked up Julia's diary once again. Julia had been on his mind over the past few days and he couldn't wait to find out more about her secret life. After turning a few pages he stopped at a passage that caught his eye.

> *I've had more visions of my past life, from before the time when I was burned. I think they all must have been from the same lifetime. At least, I looked the same. I have been concentrating on the burning so much that now I can just slip into those memories at will. It feels like passing through a veil.*
>
> *At first the memories were like whispers intruding on my sleep, wrapped in the guise of dreams, unraveling like an ethereal thread spun far back in the mists of time. But as I concentrated on them more and more I began to recall things when I was awake, just like remembering any event that has happened in this lifetime. And now I am sure that this was a real life I once lived, just as real as the one I am living now. How else could it be so vivid?*
>
> *This morning I saw myself riding a horse, alone in the forest, my long black hair flowing out behind me as I galloped. I thought the loose hair meant I was a maiden*

and for some reason that was significant, but I couldn't remember why. It felt as though I was really there, riding hard, fleeing from the wrath of someone.

I looked a bit further back in time and saw that I was engaged to be married to a British lord whom I had met only once, much to my disgust. He had asked my father for my hand in marriage and they had agreed without even consulting me. I was being sold like a slave!

The man was old and repulsive — pudgy and bald with bushy gray whiskers and rotting teeth. He had a big red nose like Uncle Ralph's and he stank as though he had never bathed in his life. His voice was loud and his manner rough. And the lecherous way he leered at me was absolutely nauseating.

I knew he was rich. That was all that mattered to my father, for my family was not well off even though we were of the nobility.

A week before the wedding I had refused to be married. I told my father I would rather run off and live in the woods than marry such a man. He took a whip and beat me, shouting that I was a disgrace to him and his entire lineage. He hollered that I had best leave off my whining and learn to honor my betters. I wasn't a girl anymore who could run about as she pleased. I was old enough to take on the duties of a wife and God help me if I refused. He wasn't about to feed me for the rest of my days when there was a perfectly able man willing to do it.

My father gave me no more chance to protest. I was locked in my room after that and he didn't allow me out until the marriage day. The day arrived all too soon. I was bathed, dressed in silk, and led out before the priest to be wed. I looked disdainfully at the men who had the audacity to force me into a marriage I didn't agree to — my father, the priest, and Lord Blackney. They were all in such good humor!

"You must be a good wife and let him have his will with you," my mother had admonished that morning. "You will grow accustomed to it. Women do. And God willing, you will have children to cheer you before long."

I glared at Lord Blackney, wondering what it was I would have to grow accustomed to, suspecting something dreadful.

I was about sixteen and quite headstrong. Certainly not one to give in to anything I didn't like, marriage or no marriage. I sulked before the priest as he spoke the words that would bind me to this revolting man for life. Schemes for escape rose one after another in my mind. I would bear what I must in silence while biding my time. Eventually there would be a chance to get away.

I knew that I would have no place in society without a man. I was considered chattel, the property of my father or husband. Without a man, I could only be a servant — or a witch. Any woman alone was suspected of that.

Yet I thought I could survive on my own somehow if I had to. Even being a servant seemed better than marriage to such a dreadful man. I fantasized about running off to live with the Romanies. I had seen their caravans passing through town and I was drawn to their colorful and free way of life. These thoughts occupied me so thoroughly that I was quite surprised when my groom lifted me in his arms and planted a hairy kiss on my mouth.

After the wedding, we were escorted to a large banquet hall at his lavish estate. A feast was laid out and I was made to sit by his side and drink wine from his cup.

This estate was to be my home for the rest of my life, yet it felt like a prison. I realized I might never see my family again and I nearly cried. But then I remembered that not one of them had taken my side against the marriage. None of them had tried to stop it. I was so angry with them, yet I dreaded the moment they would leave, fearing that I would be left alone with Lord Blackney.

But that moment had to come and when it did, it was far worse than I had feared. I was given a serving maid, a sour old thing who undressed me roughly and gave me a robe to wear. Then she left me alone in a cavernous bedroom lined with rich tapestries. I heard her speak to Lord Blackney in the hallway outside the door, telling him what a fine morsel I was. He said he would soon see for himself.

It was only a moment before he entered the bedroom. My heart froze at his nearness. He cast a quick glance at me and began to undress. I had never seen a man naked and I blushed, turning to hide my face. He laughed at me and told me to take off my robe. I couldn't move. I stood there trembling with apprehension. He had finished undressing and was moving toward me.

I must have fainted, because suddenly I found myself undressed and lying on a fur-covered bed in the middle of the room. His coarse hands scratched my tender skin and his fat bristly belly pressed down on top of me. He grunted, thrusting hard and fast, panting like a beast.

I struggled to get away, but he grabbed my hair and pulled my head back, twisting my neck until I thought it would snap. I wanted to scream, but I held back fearing more abuse. I bit my lip until I tasted blood, frantically wondering how long I would have to endure his mistreatment.

Once more I felt faint as his foul breath enveloped me, but an intense nausea rose up, much stronger than the faintness. It was only thinking of escape that prevented me from vomiting in his face. When he finally rolled off me I *could hold back no longer. I leaned over the edge of the bed and puked on the floor. I could hear him chuckle to himself as he left the room.*

It makes me so angry now when I remember it. I wish I could find that bastard and strangle him with my bare hands. Maybe it's lucky I don't know who he is in this life — if he is even alive now.

That was the first of many rapes, often accompanied by beatings when he was drunk. I was determined to get away no matter what the risk. If I saw a chance I would run. I felt that each passing day with Lord Blackney was like an eternity in hell and I thought nothing could be worse. That's how I ended up riding furiously through the woods.

Three weeks after my marriage I was finally able to escape. Blackney had left his horse by the door, saddled and ready to ride. While he was eating in the dining hall I excused myself and went to my room. It took me only a moment to tie a bundle of clothes around my waist and pull on my fur cloak, since I already had everything packed.

I walked stealthily to the door, looked around and saw no one. Silently, I crept toward the horse, untied it and leapt onto its back. Before anyone knew I was gone I had cleared the outer wall, pulling my hair free of its bindings in a symbolic rejection of my marriage. I rode hard for half an hour, then walked the horse through a stream to hide our tracks. It was a strong horse, but our mad dash had winded it severely. I knew we had to rest.

CHAPTER 10

A Bird

ঙ্গ

Tom drove pensively, winding his way down a narrow, mountain road. He was headed back to the city, leaving Julia behind in the woods once again. A car passed in the opposite direction, then suddenly a blur of feathers rolled across his windshield.

He swerved, but the little bird was dead already. It must have bounced off the oncoming car. One instant flying, the next tumbling lifelessly. Its tiny body continued to tumble in Tom's thoughts as he drove on. A body without life, yet still in motion. The idea captured his imagination, but made his heart feel heavy.

He began to ponder death, wondering how it felt to the bird to be suddenly parted from a body that went rolling on without it. There are people like that, Tom thought. Their bodies go on day after day acting out life, but when you look into their eyes you sense death. They're on autopilot, never really knowing what it is to be alive.

The bird must have felt alive, he mused. Animals always have a spark of life in their eyes. And Julia felt alive to him, even more so now that she was living so close to nature.

Tom could sense a clarity and depth in Julia beyond anything he had experienced in himself. It made him feel uneasy, fearful that he was missing out on something important. In a way, he felt more afraid of life than of death. To be alive was to constantly step into the unknown. It held the possibility of joy, but it could just as well bring pain. Julia seemed to be learning to embrace both.

It annoyed Tom to think that the joy he craved was trapped behind his fear. But what was at the root of that fear? This feeling had been with him all his life, like an original sin — a deep-seated guilt that he wanted to hide even from himself. But it was as hard to pin down as shifting light patterns in the forest.

Sometimes Tom wanted to yell out loud, but he didn't. He held back, because it seemed crazy to yell. Often he felt like Julia was prodding him, "Scream Tom, scream." Of course, that was only his imagination.

Tom projected his fear onto Julia as well as his desire. He desired Julia's love, but he was afraid to be unmasked before her, afraid to let her see the guilt that he hid in his soul. Though he didn't know why, Tom couldn't shake the feeling that he had caused Julia terrible harm. He didn't want her to find out — but maybe she already knew.

He longed for the freedom to express his true feelings, but the thought of it made him tremble inside. More than anything Tom wanted Julia's forgiveness, but for what? As far as he knew, he had never done anything to require it.

In moments of clarity, Tom could see only two choices. He could live out his life in regret, leaving things unsaid, never having taken the risk of living fully. Or he could face his irrational fear head on. He knew that's what he had to do.

His hands gripped the steering wheel with determination, turning his knuckles white as his truck swallowed pavement. Thoughts slipped into alignment as he recklessly accelerated around a bend in the road. The danger of speed brought focus, sharp and clear.

Tom knew Julia must love him in her own way, but maybe not the way he wanted. Maybe she only thought of him like a brother or a comfortable friend. She would never let him stay with her, always sending him away with a gentle smile, as if he wasn't good enough. He wondered if he could ever be good enough for her.

Now he was cruising down Interstate 5, through the wide central valley of California. Fields of rice and safflower stretched on for miles. It was a grueling four hour drive. Every Saturday he would head north to the national forest at five o'clock in the morning. He had to be back to work at his restaurant job by five in the evening.

Though he made decent money as a waiter and he didn't mind the work, the job felt like a heavy burden on top of his college coursework, plus his weekend visits to Julia. A wave of resentment washed over him as he asked himself why he was putting out all the effort in the relationship while Julia was enjoying herself on an extended vacation. It wasn't fair!

Tom had to admit, though, that Julia had never asked him to visit her. At least not since the first time. It was more like a special privilege she allowed him. When she sent him the map a few days after she disappeared, with instructions for when and where to meet her, she had asked him to bring enough food to last for several months and offered to pay him for his trouble. He had driven up the following weekend and begged her to let him visit every week. She agreed only when he promised that he would never tell anyone where she was.

On his last visit Julia had talked about her fiery visions as if they were real. It almost seemed like she expected him to remember, but he only felt an unexplained twinge of guilt. She also told him that Margaret was teaching her how to communicate with animals, plants, and even stones and nature spirits.

Maybe, Tom thought, Julia was losing her mind. She said animals and plants told her things. Something about feeling the rhythms of nature where everything was connected. Animals and plants always live in that connected space, she said, and when people enter that same consciousness they can hear their messages. Ancient people knew this, but modern humans have forgotten.

Tom was skeptical. It was hard enough communicating with Julia, let alone a deer or a tree. But somehow the way she said it made him wonder. He had watched her ask the clouds to move away from the sun and they had done exactly what she asked, but it must have been coincidence. It had to be. Clouds couldn't listen.

By the time Tom drove into the carport of his apartment building he had worked himself into a high state of angst. There were too many unknowns in his life and Julia was the biggest one. With a sigh, he climbed out of his truck and fumbled for his apartment key. He had to be at work in fifteen minutes. "Damn!" He rushed to his bedroom, pulled on his work slacks and grabbed a tie. "I never even have time to eat anymore!"

CHAPTER 11

Reflection

"I used to have dreams when I was a kid," Margaret Littlewolf said, looking thoughtfully at Julia. "Dreamed I was burning. I didn't know what they meant. They terrified me."

Julia looked up abruptly. They were sitting beside the hearth in the little forest hut, gazing at the fire. Margaret had come to visit.

"What made you say that?" Julia asked, almost holding her breath. She had suddenly dropped the stick with which she was poking the fire.

"I always think of it when I watch a fire," Margaret smiled wistfully. "A psychic once told me that it was a memory from a past life, so strong I couldn't suppress it."

"Did they go away? The dreams?" Julia asked cautiously. "You said you used to have those dreams."

"Haven't had one in a long time. Guess I didn't need the dreams anymore once I found out what they were all about." Margaret pressed her thin lips together, rocking back and forth as she gazed into the flames. "The psychic said I was burned at the stake by the Inquisition. I'd never heard of that before. Wasn't something they taught us about at the reservation school. I asked around, but nobody I knew ever heard of it. So I went to the library. They had a couple o' books that mentioned it. They called it the Spanish Inquisition. Somethin' run by the Catholic church. Said hundreds of thousands of people were tortured and burned over four hundred years — most of them women. Funny how they never talk about it."

"Funny," Julia repeated. She wasn't laughing.

"I thought ya might remember it too." Margaret glanced quickly at Julia and then back at the fire. "Is that what yer nightmares were about?"

Julia took a deep breath and sighed, nodding her head. "Yeah, I do remember. I didn't want to tell you, because I just wanted to forget about it. I haven't told anyone except Tom. Talking about it would have made it even more real."

"Ah, but it was real. In fact, I have a sense that maybe we knew each other in those days."

Julia felt as if she was being sucked back in time. "Melita?" Her vision wavered as she looked at the old woman. "Of course! That's why you feel so familiar. We did know each other! You took care of me then, just like you've been doing now."

"I like that," Margaret smiled. "It means they couldn't destroy us, or our connection. We came back and we found each other."

Julia leaned over and gave Margaret a big hug. "Thank goodness we remembered. I can't tell you how good that makes me feel."

"Yeah, me too." Margaret smiled, then frowned. "But why don't other people remember... all those people burned at the stake? Seems like more of us would remember it." She looked timeless, as if her eyes had seen centuries of history.

"It hurts too much. People don't want to remember." Julia spoke emphatically, her eyes welling with tears. "I've been so angry and full of hate. Sometimes I don't feel like I can live in such a horrible world. Like I can't take any more torment."

"So ya wanted ta die?"

Julia shook her head. "Not really. I just wanted to get away from it. I didn't care if I died or not. I didn't care about anything."

Margaret patted Julia's knee. "And now?"

"I'm not ready to go back home yet. Don't know if I ever will be, but I care now. And I don't want to die. I've learned something about being alive out here. There's always a way to make it work." She looked at her friend with gratitude. "You taught me that."

"Well, if I done nothin' else in my life I'd be happy with that. Don't you ever give up, Julia."

"I won't." Julia put her arm around the old woman and leaned her head on her shoulder. "Thank you."

Margaret looked suddenly somber. "I feel like I won't be comin' out here no more." She seemed to say it almost to herself, her dark eyes lost in the fire.

"Why not?" Julia asked, feeling a surge of alarm.

"Oh, I'd like to," Margaret answered, still gazing into the fire, "but I'm sensin' that I ain't gonna be around much longer. The next world is callin' ta me."

"But you're not even that old," Julia protested. "I mean, you're healthy. You walk a lot. You could be around for a long time."

"It's not a tragedy, dear. Death is just a part of life," Margaret smiled kindly. "You sound like ya want to fight it."

Julia shrugged. "I guess I do. Seems like I want to fight everything, doesn't it? How can you always accept things so calmly?"

"Didn't always. I was a lot like you when I was young — impulsive, headstrong and angry. I didn't know any better." The old woman's face crinkled with a smile as she went on. Her brown eyes sparkled. "I guess ya learn things as ya go along. By the time yer my age ya find out there ain't a whole lot that's worth gettin' upset about. If you're gonna have any peace inside, ya have ta accept everything and appreciate whatever comes."

"Everything?" Julia asked incredulously.

"Sure. It's all yer own reflection anyways," Margaret said. "Ain't this world just a house o' mirrors?" She paused with an encouraging smile as Julia thought about it. "Anyhow, when ya fight things ya just feed 'em an' they get stronger."

"What do you mean?" Julia asked with a frown. "How can fighting things make them stronger?"

"Because Great Spirit gives ya whatever ya ask for. An' when ya pay attention to somethin' that's just another way of askin' for it, whether ya think ya want it or not." Margaret spoke with conviction, slapping her hand on her thigh. "Great Spirit doesn't give a hang about yer yes or no. It's just yer attention that matters."

"So you're saying it's better to just ignore the things I don't like?"

"Sure am. Put your attention on somethin' ya do like, and then Great Spirit 'll send ya more o' that," Margaret asserted. She watched Julia with loving amusement, like a mother watching her baby take its first steps. "Always look fer things to appreciate, Julia. Ya can't go wrong with that," Margaret concluded.

Julia pondered this for a moment, rubbing her chin in deep concentration. Then, looking up with a hint of desperation, she asked, "But what about cruelty and abuse? What about things like being burned at the stake? How can I appreciate any of that?"

"Did ya learn anythin' from it? Anythin' 'bout yourself?"

Julia thought for a few moments, then brightened, "I'm resilient! No matter what they did to me, no matter what anyone does to me, I can't be destroyed. Wow! I never thought about it that way."

"And you're stronger fer knowin' that, " Margaret added.

"Right! I believed I was a powerless victim for that entire lifetime. I lived in fear. I didn't stand my ground; I just ran. In fact I'm still running. I still feel like a victim."

"And is that the truth? If you can't be destroyed, are you really a victim?"

Wheels were turning in Julia's head. Reality seemed to shapeshift as she felt her way into Margaret's question. "It can't be true, can it? I can't know that I'm that resilient and still feel like a victim at the same time. There's a part of me that will survive anything, no matter what they throw at me... and maybe it is just my own fear that keeps me from seeing that."

Margaret cocked her head and raised an eyebrow, looking expectantly at Julia. "What does yer heart tell ya?"

"Maybe I was never really a victim at all? Maybe I allowed myself to experience the ultimate betrayal and torture so I would have to face my false beliefs about being a victim and finally put an end to them?"

Margaret smiled, "Now yer onta something, Julia."

Suddenly kaleidoscopic images began shifting through Julia's memory — images of faces, places and events from her distant past. Romani campsites, Lord Blackney's glower, a lover's kiss, a woman's kindness, the inquisitor's leer, and flames. The woman appeared again, her face merging with Margaret's face, and Julia felt a familiar presence.

Goosebumps ran up Julia's arms. "Life is so strange, isn't it?" She shook her head. "I don't think I'll ever make sense of it."

"Well," Margaret sighed, "maybe we're not here ta make sense of it. Maybe we're just supposed ta experience it and get ta know ourselves and each other. Anyways, I'm glad I got ta know you." She patted Julia on the back. "I'd best be gettin' on my way, girl. Can't spend all day philosophizing."

Julia gave her a sad face. "I'll really miss you. And you know so much. Who will teach me when you leave? I'll be lost without you." She looked ready to cry.

"Life is yer teacher, Julia. I'm just one o' the messengers. You'll find your own answers in time."

"From your culture? Is that what I should study?"

"Well, there is deep wisdom in my culture and it could teach you a lot," Margaret replied, "but it is not yer culture. Why not look to yer own roots? Yer ancestors knew as much as mine."

"My ancestors?" Julia looked perplexed. "But they're all dead. Except my grandmother, and she doesn't seem to know much. At least not important stuff like you know."

"It's true, most of yer ancestors are gone, but they left wisdom behind. They had to hide it, 'cause them church people persecuted 'em, same as they did you an' me in our past. But the wise ones had secret ways of passin' on what they knew through stories and myths. I expect the folks livin' in yer family today never learned, but there'll always be a few wisdom keepers. Seek 'em out in books, or in person. You'll find 'em if ya look. Plus, you can still visit yer ancestors in the other world. They aren't so far away."

"I wouldn't even know how to start." Julia grumbled.

"Remember how I taught ya to listen to the plant spirits and how ya can ask 'em for help? Now ya know how ta tell which plants don't mind being picked and the ones that can heal even without being picked. It's the same thing with ancestors. They'll always be happy to answer."

"Trust my intuition. Right?"

"Yup! Just like each herb an' tree has its own healing power, each ancestor has unique wisdom ta share. Some'll be more aligned with you than others. You'll get to know 'em. Set yer intention to meet the ancestors halfway — in yer dreams and trance journeys. They'll show up.

"Yer wisdom-keeper ancestors were Irish bards and druids. They hid what they knew in legends that started out as stories told aloud. Some o' those stories were collected and written in books. You can find 'em today in libraries and bookstores."

"You mean fairytales?"

"Those too, if the tales are old enough — always look fer the oldest roots of any story. But what I mean are the ancient Irish and Welsh myths and even the legends of King Arthur — stories about gods and goddesses and faeries."

"Faeries?" Julia was surprised. "Do they really exist?"

"You'll have to discover that fer yerself, Julia." Margaret twinkled. "Celtic lore is full of 'em, but I can't give ya all the answers. It's like a treasure hunt. And don't forget to ask fer help. The ancestors can't help ya if you don't ask. I'm sure you'll find what ya need. And," Margaret paused, glancing at Julia with an impish smile, "you just might discover that some of yer ancestors are faeries. Think about that fer a bit!"

The girl fell silent for a few moments. Then she looked intently at Margaret. "So — how old are you, anyway?"

"I reckon I'll be ninety-two next birthday," Margaret answered, jutting out her wrinkled chin. "That's old enough."

"No way! You don't look anywhere near that old," Julia exclaimed.

Margaret just grinned, her brown eyes crinkling as she patted Julia softly on the knee. "I love ya, girl."

She kissed Julia's forehead, then picked up her backpack, slung it over one shoulder and walked out the door.

That was the last time Julia saw Margaret Littlewolf. Maybe the old woman had died, or maybe she wasn't strong enough to go for long walks in the woods anymore. Julia missed her a lot. Margaret had made it clear that she was leaving for good this time. It was hard to believe that someone that old could be so full of life and good humor. And now she was gone.

Margaret had talked about the burning times. That mattered more than anything to Julia. There was someone else who remembered. Julia no longer felt alone. She wasn't imagining things and she could finally let go of the fear that she was going crazy. Someone else had dreamed the same dreams — someone who lived to be old and wise and very happy. That was a great inspiration.

CHAPTER 12

Jealousy

A fter reading that last section of Julia's diary, Ralph felt strangely agitated. An inexplicable unease moved like a shadow in his soul. His pulse was racing as he closed the little book and he was determined never to open it again.

It wasn't her candid description of the rape that bothered him. It was where she wrote, "It makes me so angry when I remember it. I wish I could find that bastard and strangle him with my bare hands. I guess it's lucky I don't know who he is in this life — if he is even alive now." It chilled Ralph to the bone, though he couldn't fathom why.

It had never occurred to him that Julia could be dangerous, but then he supposed anyone could be if pushed far enough. Assuming that the whole story was made up in her head, Ralph had to wonder what could have triggered so much rage. As far as he knew, Julia was a virgin. So where did the outrage about the rape come from? Ralph wondered if something had happened to her that she kept secret.

Of course Tom had always been around, but Julia seemed to keep him at arm's length. It was obvious that she liked him and the two of them spent a lot of time together, but they had grown up together from infancy. Their mothers had been best friends. To Ralph, they seemed more like siblings than lovers.

He wondered how Julia could have imagined a man like Lord Blackney so clearly. It didn't make sense. Then, with a chill, it dawned on him that she might not have imagined him at all. That is when he had to stop reading. Her words suffocated him.

As a devout Catholic, Ralph had always believed that people went to heaven after they died — or purgatory if they weren't pure enough for heaven yet. He figured he would have to spend some time in purgatory to pay for his sins, but he would eventually make it to heaven. Of course, if someone was really bad they would end up in hell, but he guessed there wouldn't be many people monstrous enough to deserve eternal damnation.

The only other option the Catholic church offered for the afterlife was limbo. That was for good people who were unbaptized, but he wondered about that. If God was fair, which Ralph sometimes questioned, how could an innocent child be stuck in limbo forever, just because it had died before being baptized? Limbo was the edge of hell, according to one definition he'd read. He hated to think of all the unbaptized babies being dumped there, along with all the people who had never even had the opportunity to learn about baptism.

It was all because of original sin, whatever that was. Ralph wondered what sort of sin a baby could commit that would bar it from heaven. Maybe the very fact of being human was a sin, but why would God create humans to be born in sin, even if their ancestors had been sinful? Wouldn't everyone deserve to have a fresh start?

Ralph was beginning to feel nauseated as he always did when he questioned church doctrines. It was important to him to feel sure of his beliefs. He needed clear answers he could rely on, but the more he thought about these things, the muddier the answers seemed to get.

Reincarnation was not something he had ever considered and the thought of it scared the heck out of him. It was something he couldn't be sure about and that filled him with angst. He needed to be sure.

But hell scared him even more, so he made sure not to miss Mass on Sundays or holy days of obligation, and he went to confession regularly. He didn't want to find himself facing death with a mortal sin on his soul. That was a one-way ticket straight to hell, and missing Sunday Mass was one of the mortal sins.

Ralph knew he wasn't perfect, but he trusted that God would forgive his faults as long as he tried to follow the rules of his church to the best of his ability. That was the whole point of religion, he figured. You could be a flawed human being and still be welcomed into heaven after death if you sought forgiveness.

But now something was eating away at the foundations of his beliefs. After reading Julia's diary, unwelcome questions invaded his mind. Could Julia's stories actually be true? It seemed preposterous, yet Julia seemed to have no doubt that she had lived before. And what if he had lived another life that he didn't even remember?

These questions continued to haunt him until curiosity got the better of him. Ralph's resolve to stop reading the diary lasted only two days. He wondered if Carmen had been burned for the crime of deserting her husband — or were there darker deeds to come? Surprised at the intensity of his interest, he was again sucked into the whirl of Julia's distant past.

I lay down that night beneath an elder bush, wrapped in my fur cloak. Blackney's horse was tethered close by. It was cool, but spring had warmed the ground. Before long I was too deep in sleep to notice any discomfort. I woke early as the sun streaked the sky crimson. After rolling up my cloak, I climbed wearily into the saddle. It was going to be a long ride before I reached a town.

I passed several men working in their fields who looked at me suspiciously. A disheveled woman riding alone in fine clothes was a rare sight. I inquired after the Romanies, for I had seen a band of them passing by my husband's house on the day of my wedding and I hoped they would not have gone far. I had money to give them if they would take me in, gold and silver stolen from my husband's purse. He was a wealthy man, but he could not buy me with his riches.

Once I reached a town, I traded my rich gowns for peasant's frocks and a thick gray cloak of wool. Blackney's horse and saddle I traded for another just as fine and food to last me a week. I wanted to keep nothing that could be recognized by anyone who sought me. At last I felt free, but for the lingering unwholesome feeling that Lord Blackney had left his mark on me. My heart ached for my lost innocence.

There was a fortune teller in the town square and I gave her my hand to read, along with a copper piece. She looked into my eyes and laughed.

"You have the sight," she said. "One day you will do what I do." She paused, looking at me thoughtfully. "But what is it you want to know right now?"

I didn't understand. "Can you not tell my fortune?" I questioned her with annoyance. "I need your help."

"That you do, little one," she murmured, gazing at my palm with a furrowed brow. "I see flames." She waved her hand before her as she spoke. "But not now. First you will become one of us. Is that what you seek?"

"Yes. Can you take me in? I have money."

She nodded. "I will ask. Come with me. My name is Melita," she said, smiling.

I followed her into the woods to her vardo, the colorful horse-drawn wagon where she made her home. Nearby there were several other vardos, all painted with intricate designs.

Melita winked at me and made her way past a string of piebald horses that nickered and snorted at her approach. She crossed a road, motioning me to stay where I was. There was an older man to whom she spoke in hushed tones, and soon other men had gathered and were looking my way. One who was young and handsome seemed particularly interested.

After a few moments Melita returned. "We will take you in and teach you for two years and then you must leave us — alone." She put special emphasis on the last word, but it wasn't until later that I realized what she meant.

Strangely, though all this took place in an unfamiliar language, I can now understand it easily and translate it into English as it comes into my memory.

I was not long with the Romanies when I noticed that my menses had stopped. This worried me and I spoke to Melita who had taken me under her wing. She looked at me knowingly and asked if I had been with a man. I told her of my marriage and the escape I had made after three weeks.

"Just as I suspected," Melita said.

That explained it as far as she was concerned, but I was still confused. She told me I was with child. She had sensed it right away. That is why she had offered to take me in. Without a husband I could hardly raise a child myself. The Romanies were offering to raise it as one of their own. It would grow up as a Traveler and never know of its noble blood. I smiled bitterly. That would serve Lord Blackney right.

Melita's son, Leo, was the one who had looked at me with interest on that first day and now he dared to come closer. I liked him right away. He was a little older than I was, perhaps nineteen, with unruly dark hair and eyes as black as jet. He bred horses with his father and sold them in towns they passed through — the finest cob horses that his people had been raising for generations. They were compact and muscular with luxurious flowing manes and feathered feet.

On the day his father's best mare was to be bred Leo took my hand and led me to the clearing where the horses were tied. His father was there and another man I had never seen. The new man had brought a silver-gray stallion that was stamping and whinnying loudly as we came close.

Leo's father held the mare on a tether, leading her to meet her mate.

The force with which the stallion reared broke his halter, but the man holding him only grinned, knowing that escape was far from the animal's mind. It mounted the mare forcefully, biting her neck as she trembled beneath his weight. As I watched, I felt my face flush.

Leo's dark eyes sparkled as he glanced at me. I looked away. This was the way babies were made. Every peasant knew it, but I had been raised in a vacuum. I now realized with a wave of anger why my husband had used me so roughly. He only wanted children, a son to inherit his estate, but I wasn't about to be bred like some mare with no choice in the matter.

It galled me even more now that I knew he had gotten his way. There was indeed a child growing in my belly, planted there by his seed, but he would never know it. That gave me some small satisfaction.

I turned away and stomped back toward the camp. In a moment I heard Leo's footsteps behind me, running to catch up. He looked at me slyly when he reached my side.

"Were you bored already?" He cocked his head impudently. When I didn't answer he went on. "I find it exciting to watch horses mating, do you not? Or perhaps it reminds you too much of yourself?"

"I looked at him warily. "Why would it remind me of myself? I am not a horse."

He patted my belly. "Mother told me you were with child, so you must have done what those horses were doing."

"I did nothing!" I protested furiously, stamping my foot. "It was forced on me by a husband I detested and I escaped at my first opportunity."

Leo looked impressed. Then his face went soft and he moved closer to me. "That is sad. It could have been such a pleasure if only you were with a better man."

"Ha!" I tossed my head defiantly. "One man could only be as bad as another in that way."

"Do not be so sure." His voice was tender and his eyes were teasing. "Do you think I could not make you feel it as a pleasure?"

I looked at him incredulously and he touched my cheek very softly. I began to quiver inside. "No, I do not think anyone could," I answered him, but I wondered.

"Let me try," he teased again with a tiny smile. "It is the perfect time. You cannot get another child when there is one already. And if you do not find it pleasurable I will stop at your word. I promise."

I looked at him thoughtfully. No man had ever spoken to me with such respect and openness. His eyes were eager, yet gentle. I wanted him to touch me, just as softly as before, but what my husband had done I would never allow. I felt I would die of humiliation.

He read my eyes and touched my cheek again, slowly moving closer. Our lips met before I could move away. I was surprised at the softness of his mouth. He kissed me again and again until I melted into his arms wanting him never to stop. Nothing had ever felt so wonderful.

Then he pulled back with a mischievous grin. "That is only a small taste of the pleasure I can give you." He winked, smacked my behind, and turned toward the clearing where his father was working with the horses. "Come to me when you are ready for more," he said as he chuckled over his shoulder.

I watched him walk away with a pounding heart. After that I thought about him always, longing for his kisses, but afraid he would ask for more. His ebony eyes haunted me.

It was a whole week before I saw him again and I was ready to melt into his arms. His kisses were like a healing balm.

Then there was another miserable week apart from him, and another after only a brief meeting. By that time I was ready to give him anything he wanted, but he made me wait. His tenderness and restraint drove me mad with desire.

A few weeks later I found myself lying naked beside him, amazed at the delicious feelings he aroused. I could hear my mother's words again. "You must let him have his will with you." I obeyed now, surrendering, feeling waves of ecstasy break over me, rushing in wild torrents through my veins.

Then a delicious peace descended. A hint of honeysuckle drifted on the breeze. It was a moment of perfection.

Ralph slammed the diary shut, flushing with irritation. How dare she go off with some Gypsy boy in the woods and give herself to him as if she were not a married woman. The boy was only using her. Couldn't she see that?

He threw the diary to the floor and jumped to his feet to pace the room, fuming. That little slut! He felt like giving her a good slap. He would certainly give her a piece of his mind if he ever saw her again.

As he returned to his seat, shaking with rage, Ralph caught a glimpse of himself in the mirror across the room. His face was twisted and flushed, reflecting the turmoil inside. But why was he so angry?

Certainly, it wasn't Julia who had done anything to deserve his anger. She may have had a vivid imagination. She may even have remembered things from another lifetime. But he was angry with a girl who had lived and died hundreds of years ago, because she made love with a Romani lad. Ralph was beginning to realize that he was actually feeling jealous.

Jealousy made no sense to him. It did not fit into his life in any way. There were no women to be jealous over. Women avoided him and he mistrusted them. They could never live up to his expectations of perfection. And perhaps they were perceptive enough to see the homeliness of his heart. Whatever the reason, the opportunity to be jealous had never presented itself, yet he could not deny that he felt it now.

CHAPTER 13

Solitude

Julia hadn't expected to wrestle with loneliness in her search for inner peace. She had longed for solitude. Yet, though it was easy enough to live in the woods by herself, without someone to share it with she often felt desolate.

Maybe it was because she missed Tom. Seeing him for a few hours once a week just wasn't enough. Not that she was in love with him, but she did feel a strong attachment. After all, he had been her best friend since early childhood. He might be the only friend she had left. Julia wanted to take him in her arms and keep him close and she knew he wanted that even more than she did.

She closed her eyes, visualizing his chiseled features and brilliant green eyes that gleamed like tourmaline fire. There was such innocence in those eyes, and so much fear. Maybe he was afraid that she would see his vulnerability and laugh. That might have been Tom's greatest fear, yet it gave her power. She could crush him with a laugh, but she wouldn't do it. She knew too well how it could wound.

Perhaps that is the fear of every man, Julia thought. Cruelty, domination and violence are all smoke screens to hide that frail place within. But Tom was not violent or cruel. He had more gentle smoke screens, like looking away when he felt the intensity of her gaze, or hesitating just a bit too long when she asked him how he felt.

As darkness fell that night Julia drifted on the edge of sleep, aware of a vast emptiness around her, an eerie silence. There are different kinds of silences in nature. She had noticed that in her first days in the woods. This night the silence was full, weighed down with its burden, ready to burst. Even the air felt restless. She imagined herself poised between worlds, sinking slowly into the realm of dreams.

Suddenly, she found herself wide awake and sitting bolt upright on her cot. Had she heard a sound or only dreamed it? She listened intently. It was probably just an animal and she had nothing to fear. Why then, did she feel as if she were in danger?

She peered out through a crack in the wall of her hut, seeing only stillness in the faint moonlight. Then suddenly a flash of lightning illuminated the trees, followed quickly by booming thunder. Julia laughed with relief. It was only a storm — the first of the season. And what a storm it was! In the stillness between claps of thunder she heard the slow patter of huge raindrops hitting the tin roof. Moments later a downpour crashed through the trees in seamless sheets. Rain poured in through cracks in the ceiling, drenching her bed. It was cold. Again, Julia wished Tom was there with her.

This was a new feeling. In all the months she had lived in the woods, she had never been afraid. Now when a moment of fear touched her, she found herself wishing for Tom. He would make her feel safe. Or perhaps he would only make her feel that the danger could not separate her from him. Maybe she had always been afraid of that, but she pretended to be strong.

She had wanted to lure Tom into exposing his vulnerable side, but she hid hers even from herself. Now she was definitely feeling vulnerable. She had never felt it in such a visceral way before. Julia had been saving her vulnerability to share in a special moment, like a prize.

It wasn't a prize, she realized now. It was herself, feeling alone in the forest, hearing strange noises in the night. Her life felt fragile as a twig, and suddenly all around her she heard twigs snapping in the wind. She put dry wood on the fireplace grate and blew the glowing embers to life. For a long time she sat huddled by the fire, wrapped in her damp sleeping bag and listening to the wind.

When she woke the next morning, Julia found herself lying beside the hearth in a puddle of water. The fire had died and the world outside was silent once again. With a moan, she pulled herself up and rummaged through her backpack for dry clothes. It took some time to get the fire burning again. Everything was wet, including most of the matches, but she found one dry matchbook in the pocket of her jacket. With a bit of coaxing she got a cheery blaze burning and warmth quickly filled the hut. Her soaked sleeping bag hung dripping beside the fireplace, wisps of steam rising from its surface.

Outside, the sky had cleared and the autumn sun filtered weakly through bare branches overhead. Winter was fast approaching. Julia had learned enough from Margaret Littlewolf to survive there through the winter. She even had some hazy past-life memories of how the Romanies had done it. There was nothing she couldn't manage. Still, the thought of dealing with storms and cold for a whole winter made her long for the comforts of civilization.

Something had shifted overnight. The adventure, which at first seemed like an escape from the horrors of her past and had then become simply fun, was quickly losing its appeal. There was more she wanted from life than this. Much more. She wanted not to be alone. She wanted love and companionship.

It was a week since she had last seen Tom and that meant he would be visiting again that day. Each visit left her feeling more dissatisfied than the last. Maybe it was finally time to think about returning to the city. Going back to Uncle Ralph's house was unthinkable, but she didn't want to move in with Tom, either. There was only one other possibility, since she wouldn't be able to rent her own place until she found a job. Grandma would have to put her up for awhile.

For the first time in weeks, Julia allowed herself to think of life back home. In her mind Ralph loomed larger than ever. He probably still lived alone, as he had always done before she moved in with him. Nobody seemed to love him, really. In spite of his amorous desires, his personal habits were sure to keep intimacy away. He wanted the touch, but not the complexities of love.

He wanted women, but not their depth of feeling, the part that made them alive and of course unpredictable. More than anything he seemed afraid of losing someone he had grown attached to. A real woman could run off whenever she wished. He had no control. Even Julia had run off. Safer were the images of women posing for him on the pages of his magazines. They could never escape.

It made Julia's skin crawl to think of Ralph. She could see his washed-out, gray eyes peering at her when he thought she wasn't looking. He was so homely. Pale and balding with patches of rusty hair over his ears and that red knob of a nose. Why had he taken her in, anyway? It wasn't like he was fond of children. He didn't really seem to be fond of anyone, for that matter — except maybe his snails, she thought with a smirk.

With a shudder, she put Ralph out of her mind and focused on the rich smell of wet rotting leaves. Overhead a raven called in a deep throaty croak. She looked up and smiled, grateful for a friendly voice in a melancholy moment.

CHAPTER 14

Frank Davis

᭝ᬄ

The nice thing about quitting is that you don't have to worry about responsibilities anymore. Someone else can pay the bills, balance the checkbook, hold down the job. You're through. That's the way Frank Davis thought about it as he wandered along the edge of a country road. Autumn was in the air, crisp and cool. It felt like a good time to make a change.

In a field beside the road he saw a bunch of tiny calves huddled together, bleating for their mothers. They were the lucky ones, he thought. At least they would live long enough to pay for their keep in milk. The males were caged somewhere inside, awaiting their turn at the slaughterhouse. Strange world.

Frank had been a dairyman up until that morning, but that last veal calf really got to him — a little Jersey who looked at him with the most mournful brown eyes he had ever seen. He had hardened his heart to that look so many times, but he just couldn't do it anymore. It seemed as if the little thing had trusted him. He filled the milk bottle with artificial milk and gave it to the calf. Apologized that he couldn't do more. Then he just walked out. He never even picked up his paycheck.

It was a rash move. He had no place to go, having lived in a cabin there at the dairy. And now he didn't even have enough money to rent another place. He walked along the road feeling oddly unburdened. Destitute, yet there was a joy unleashed in him that more than made up for the security he had thrown away. After all, what did it matter, really? He was an invisible speck walking on a minuscule planet in the midst of a vast universe. He winced at the thought, his mood suddenly shifting.

What if we were all alone here, drifting through space like microbes on a marble dropped by some thoughtless Titan? That was a disturbing possibility. If there were other civilizations out there, if only he could know it for sure, existence wouldn't feel so random.

Even time is only relative to our experience of the sun and moon moving across the sky, he thought. Ultimately, there is nothing real about it. Eternity would never change, even after our sun has long burned itself out. Nothing could affect eternity.

Frank walked on, amusing himself with such thoughts, trying to imagine an infinite universe, or the eternal existence of his soul. When he was a child he had gone to church and learned about eternal damnation. To him that meant an eternity of trying to understand eternity. That was the worst hell he could imagine. Even now as he walked, thinking about it left him with an agitated churning in his gut. He wouldn't be able to sleep until he forced it out of his mind.

There were only two possibilities at the end of life, oblivion or eternal consciousness. Both of them terrified him. To cease to exist was an awful option. How could he not be while the whole universe went on without him? And yet the idea of going on and on and on with no end possible, ever, that tied his guts in knots. He worked himself into a dither trying to imagine first the one alternative and then the other, finally concluding that it would be such a relief to die. Although, he realized with a shudder, it might be no relief at all.

He looked around and sighed. Sweet Mother Earth and all the myriad growing things still called to him. He couldn't leave her yet. He almost felt as though Earth needed him. She had to exist in this unfathomable universe too. That gave him comfort.

Frank couldn't understand why people abused planet Earth. He wanted to rescue her. She needed to be respected, even loved. Yes, he actually felt that he loved her, not that he would ever say such a thing to anyone else. It sounded so touchy-feely. But in his heart it was the truth.

He took a deep breath and stretched out his arms to the sky. There were rituals moving in his veins, but he didn't know how to express them. Dionysus danced in his heart. Indeed, he was on the edge of ecstasy. To exist forever in such bliss would not be so bad.

It was only when he became aware of his separateness that dread would tear at him. In ecstasy his soul expanded out in all directions, straining to meet and meld with everything other. That's how he discovered the reality that there was no other.

Otherness was the illusion from which he could learn who he was — just his own reflection. He had to remember it wasn't real. If he forgot, he would be drawn into self-destructive habits, like indulging in drugs and booze. Those had made him their prisoner for too many years. He felt proud for extricating himself from their grip. It had taken a great strength of will to break free and now he was determined never to go back.

Frank headed north, walking slowly with his thumb out, hoping for a ride. He could always find work cutting firewood up there if nothing else presented itself. Now that winter was approaching there would be a big demand for cord wood.

After that he might go back to the city. He had friends there who would help him get a job. They were constantly entreating him to settle down in the city, but country life kept calling him back. He needed the outdoors. Nature had something to offer that he could never find in a city — hope. In the midst of that sprawl of gray buildings, honking cars, and human desperation he lost it. Depression curled in on him like a poison smoke that would choke out his life. He couldn't handle that for long.

The sound of a vehicle slowing down behind him pulled his mind back to the present. He turned to find a beat-up Chevy truck approaching. The driver was a good-looking young guy who jerked his head sideways, signaling him to climb aboard. Frank was almost annoyed at the interruption, but quickly realized his good fortune. There had been times when he had to stand out on the road for three days before anyone would pick him up.

He grinned appreciatively and introduced himself as he slid onto the seat beside the driver. The kid's name was Tom and he said he was on his way to visit a friend who was camping up north. Strange time of year for camping, Frank thought. Some people would try anything.

Tom seemed lost in his own thoughts, so Frank returned to his earlier musings. He watched the countryside slip by outside his window and thought about eternity. Frightening as that was, the idea of spending it alone was much worse. In this earthly life he felt a longing to touch the soul of another, to form a bond that could never be broken no matter if death or time intervened. Perhaps death was as much an illusion as time, he reflected. It would have to be if those bonds were to hold fast through the endlessness of eternity.

Frank was afraid he might miss out on that sort of connection and he'd find himself totally cut off and eternally alone. But he had a habit of cutting himself off. When he felt bonds begin to form he became unnerved. As soon as he started to feel close to any other being he had to run. It was the same with a woman as it was with a calf. The moment he felt someone creeping into his heart he would panic. It was all he could do to convince himself that he didn't care, but he managed it every time.

Before the dairy there was a woman. Someone tender, understanding and open. She invaded him with her sweetness. One morning he awoke at her side while she was still sleeping. He felt like she was breathing inside of him. With a pang he realized that he was so close to her he couldn't tell where he left off and she began. It was as though she had projected tentacles of soul stuff into his heart and he had no way of loosening them. Of course he was not afraid of her. She was gentle as a lamb. It was something in himself that scared him.

The intimacy. There was that open place in his soul through which the hollow winds of eternity might blow. He had let her in. She didn't force her way, but once she was there, so close inside of him, he felt as though he was dying.

Maybe he would have died in a sense if he hadn't left her that day. He would have had to make a choice between accepting that feeling of death, or punishing her. He couldn't do either, so he left.

This intimacy, which scared him enough to leave the woman he loved, was not sexual. Romantic passion and physical closeness presented no problem. That was as close and as vulnerable as he had any intention of being with anyone — but life did not always follow his intentions.

CHAPTER 15

Isobel

It took a few days for Ralph to get back to reading Julia's diary. He was finally cooling off over her affair with the Romani boy. Why he should be so upset was a mystery to him, but having been rejected by so many women in his life, he could identify strongly with the jilted husband. The poor guy was probably bound by the church to honor the marriage and he couldn't take another wife until he had proof that the first was dead. Meanwhile, Ralph fumed to himself, his wife was off having the time of her life with the heathen Gypsies.

Ralph had resolved, this time, that he would not get worked up over the diary. It was wreaking havoc with his blood pressure. But curiosity ate holes in his resolve. There was a part of him that actually wanted to see her burn. He wanted to get to that part of her story and find out why.

Sitting at the kitchen table with his morning coffee, he began to leaf through the diary between bites of scrambled eggs and toast. He skimmed over a lot of stuff about school dances and who was in love with her that week. She seemed not to care, only to make a note of it with amusement. What a heartbreaker she was!

When he came upon the continuation of her story, he began to read avidly.

> *I'm skipping over the boring months of my pregnancy, aside from a few details of interest. The Romanies were*

wonderful teachers, and I also met a healer who sometimes came to our camp to trade herbs and remedies with Melita. It was from her that I learned the art of seeing the future, an art I still possess in this lifetime. She told me I had an inborn talent. I only needed to learn how to use it. Soon I was going into towns with the tinkers and horse traders to ply my trade. People were willing to pay me well and when they discovered that my predictions were accurate they came again and again.

I continued to carry on my love affair with Leo, Melita's son. Even as I bulged with child he still wanted me. But then, as the birth time grew close, he told me that we would have to stop once the baby came. He could not risk making another child. That shocked me. I had begun to hope that he would stay with me, but the Romanies stuck with their own kind. It would undermine their whole way of life if they began to intermarry with gaujos.

I knew then what Melita had meant when she told me I would have to go alone when I left them. No Romani would go with me anymore than I could stay. I was not one of them. I felt sad, naturally, but I understood. When Leo was married later that year to a girl his father had chosen, I kissed him on the cheek and wished him well. We were friends.

My child was born in late winter, a girl with eyes as blue as the sky and hair the color of mouse fur. Lord Blackney's coloring. It was an easy labor. I had been given tea of raspberry leaves and other herbs that Melita thought I needed in preparation. I was fit as well from all the walking I did every day. Scarcely three hours of labor had gone by when my daughter slipped into Melita's capable hands. I named her Isobel.

I felt all of a mother's devotion, even as I determined that the child would stay with Melita. For a year and a quarter I would nurse her and care for her and then I would have to go. I couldn't subject my child to the rigors of survival with a single mother in a hostile world. Better that she stay where it was safe. Still, it broke my heart to think of the day I would have to leave her behind.

I thought of Lord Blackney often then. This child of his, whom he would never know, brought back his memory more clearly than I had felt it since I ran from his house. She was half English, and a Lady in fact. Blackney was from Britain before he came to Spain. I wondered what had made him leave his native country. There was so little I knew about him.

My tiny Isobel would wonder who her father was. Perhaps she even had a right to know. And yet, she would be so much happier if she never asked — if she lived as a Romani and became one of them. Would they tell her she must go one day when she was grown, just as they had done with me? Melita said no, but how could she be sure? The lines between races seemed to be so clearly drawn.

My daughter was already walking when it came time for me to leave. She was beginning to say words and would greet me with a happy "Ma!" whenever she saw me. I tried to separate myself more and more from her once she was weaned and she grew close to Melita, as if she were her true grandmother. I was glad to see it.

When at last the dreaded day arrived, I held my Isobel so tightly that she squirmed out of my arms and ran to Melita. That was what I wanted. I told myself it was, yet my heart would not listen. As I turned to walk away tears were streaming down my face.

I picked up my belongings from the back of the little vardo that I had shared with Melita. It would be my daughter's home now, perhaps for all her life. I had walked so many miles behind it, running my eyes over its intricate *designs with their bright colors. It was forever engraved in my mind. I liked to think of Isobel living there.*

Leo was watching when I lifted my heavy pack and headed for the road. A fine cob mare stamped restlessly at his side. He walked up to me with a sad smile and reached out to take my hand, passing the mare's reins to me. I looked at him in surprise and he kissed me briefly on the lips. It had been so long since he, or any man, had touched me that I felt faint with excitement. I looked curiously into his raven-black eyes.

"To remember me, Carmen," he nodded at the horse. "She is the finest alive, just as you are. Her name is Sloe and she belongs with you."

I flushed. Leo had never given me reason to think he still loved me. He was utterly faithful to his new wife. But now this. The mare was surely his favorite.

"I could not, Leo. It is too great a gift."

"Please," his dark eyes pleaded. "I will be offended if you refuse."

I bowed my head in gratitude and then looked at him painfully. "I will always love you, Leo. Thank you so much."

He embraced me with such fervor that my knees trembled. One last kiss and he was gone. I watched as he blended slowly into the forest shadows. The horse he had given me was jet black.

CHAPTER 16

Lucky

"So tell me about this friend of yours," Frank struck up a conversation with Tom as they sped along the highway. "How long has he been camping out? Must be getting pretty cold at night by now."

Tom laughed. "*She* has been out there all summer. I visit her every week, but she's never wanted to go back with me. I guess she's just adapted to it by now."

"She's camping all by herself?" Frank was impressed. "Some woman!"

"Well, she was staying with a Native American woman at first, but I guess she went back to her family. They live on a reservation somewhere nearby." Tom shrugged as if it was inconsequential. "Anyway, Julia's got a lot of guts, but I suspect she's running away from something." He looked sideways at Frank with a conspiratorial grin. "You want to meet her, don't you? She's got you curious." Tom was feeling a little proud. Wanting to show her off.

Frank rubbed the stubble on his chin. "I'd be game. I haven't got any other plans. She your girl?"

"I don't know." Tom sighed with a shake of his head. "I mean I'm working on it. She's a hard one to pin down. But," he gave a quick laugh, "we've known each other all our lives, since we were babies, so she's kind of like a sister. That makes it sort of weird."

"Maybe you're lucky then," Frank chuckled, half to himself.

"What do you mean, lucky?"

Frank looked down at his callused hands. "Once you catch a woman you spend the rest of your life trying to hold your own space. They have a way of crawling inside of you, wanting to share your soul. It spooks me. I can't handle it."

"Well, it seems like it would work both ways. They must feel the same thing about men. It seems like Julia does anyway."

"Maybe so, but they're designed that way. I mean — could you imagine having a baby growing inside of you? That's got to be strange. It must feel more natural to them, ya know. But, eh —" He waved his hand as if to drive the thought away. "I just can't think about it. It's probably just me."

Tom thought for a moment before he answered. "Yeah, I guess most guys don't think about it too much. They just go for it."

Frank issued a snort of amusement then fell silent. Tom was now reassessing his relationship with Julia in a new light. He had been longing to get close to her, to merge so completely that he could never lose her. Now he began to wonder if that was what he really wanted. He had never even thought of the possibility of being too close.

They sped past small towns and farmlands and into the thick of the forest, each lost in their own thoughts. The air smelled fresh with a hint of damp leaf mold and fir needles. Long lines of migrating Canada geese streaked across the sky, heading south for the winter, honking loudly as they passed overhead. Tom felt strangely exhilarated. He looked across at Frank who seemed to be dozing off.

Julia would be surprised if he showed up with a stranger. Or maybe she wouldn't. It was hard to know about her. How much she could foresee, or not, was a matter of intense curiosity to Tom. He tried to take it lightly, but there was something unsettling about being around a person who just knew things out of the blue.

Her eyes seemed to penetrate to the core of everything they touched, including himself. He felt exposed even by the memory of her gaze. Sometimes he wondered if he loved her at all. Maybe it was just some kind of spell that she cast over him that made it impossible to tear himself away.

Frank roused himself with a grunt as the truck veered off the main road. "You taking me with you?"

"Might as well," Tom shrugged. "You wanted to meet her, didn't you?" It was only at that moment that he made the decision to take Frank along. He wasn't in the mood to ponder it too much.

"Didn't think you'd take it seriously. I mean, I don't want to horn in on your party or anything, you know."

"No problem. Besides, where else would you go? I can't just dump you off in the middle of nowhere. I'll give you a ride up to the next town on my way out. It's only about ten miles north of here."

"Hey, you're all right. I appreciate it, man."

"It's nothing." Tom shrugged, deftly guiding the truck down the rutted, one-lane road. He could hardly wait to see Julia.

CHAPTER 17

Transition

൭ඁ൙

Julia shuffled through drifts of multicolored leaves, feeling invigorated by the crispness of the air. She was heading toward the clearing near the road where she always met Tom. Autumn awakened a sense of wonder in her, along with a bittersweet awareness of life's transitory nature. A wave of nostalgia came over her as she walked, because it felt like an ending. She carried her backpack and sleeping bag and a few pretty stones and feathers she had collected in the woods. Everything else was left behind. At last she had made the decision to go home.

She felt more like a woman than a girl now, as though her time in the woods had signaled a ritual passage from one stage of life to another. It was a subtle change, hard to define, but she found herself feeling ripe and ready for experience. Ready to love and be loved. She looked forward to Tom's arrival with a newfound sense of maturity.

She had a richer sense of reality now, and an expansion of wisdom from which to draw as she moved through life. Her months with Margaret Littlewolf had brought her to a place of balance and serenity unlike anything she had ever known before. She finally felt at peace with the anguish of her past life and she was beginning to understand it in a new way.

It would be a long time before she'd be ready to face Uncle Ralph again, but at least she didn't hate him anymore. Forgiveness was another matter entirely. What he had done in her former life was unforgivable, and in this life, the lecherous way he treated women made her skin crawl.

But now she was ready to start a whole new phase in her life — a phase that didn't include Ralph. Perhaps she was even ready to take a leap into a romantic relationship with Tom. She knew that is what he had been hoping for. Maybe the day had come.

How odd then that when she spotted Tom standing on the hilltop by the road, her heart overflowing with the intention of exploring a deeper connection, she stopped suddenly in shock. He wasn't alone! She felt betrayed. He had promised never to tell anyone where she was, and now this. How could she expose her most vulnerable desires and fears to him with this stranger as a witness? It just wouldn't work. A cool reserve swept over her and her face became an impassive mask. She stood rooted to her spot and, for the first time, Tom noticed her before she reached him.

Frank had already spotted her and he stood awestruck at the sight. Her flaming hair, caught up in the wind, was whirling around a fire in her eyes. But it only lasted for an instant. She changed in a flash as a fog settled over her and the glow in her face turned ashen.

Frank knew then that he didn't belong there. He had caused that change and it stabbed him with remorse. Without hesitating, he spun on his heel and ran back toward the truck. He felt as if he had trespassed on some intimate territory he wasn't meant to see. More than that he felt as if he had stumbled into his own destiny and it terrified him.

"Wait!" Julia shouted at the top of her lungs. She dashed forward. Tom ran toward her, joyful in his passion to reach her, to throw his arms around her. She sprinted past him with a crazed look in her eyes.

"Julia?" Tom called out, whirling to face her as she ran by. He felt empty, lost, as he watched her dash away.

Frank stopped abruptly at the truck, panting. Julia reached him in a moment.

"Why did you run away?" she demanded, breathing heavily, her amber eyes flashing. Their eyes met in an explosion of light.

"Uh — I, I don't really know," he admitted. "I just knew I didn't belong there. I mean I don't belong here." He stood eyeing her defiantly, grizzled, tough, and very much aware of his quivering heart.

He wasn't a handsome man. His lips were a bit too large, his eyebrows too bushy, but the deep blue of his eyes made her forget his deficiencies — deep as the twilight sky. Julia was transfixed. Though she had decided intellectually that Tom had all the qualities she was looking for in a man, beauty, strength, gentleness, dependability and all the rest, this man had something she had never even put into the equation. Pure animal magnetism.

"I know you," she said with a sudden realization. "I'm not sure exactly how yet, but it will come to me."

"I don't think so," Frank answered. "You are not one I'd forget." He eyed her with a mixture of wariness and curiosity.

She touched his arm lightly and turned, indicating that he should follow as she led the way back to Tom, who watched in deep confusion.

"I'd like to be introduced to your friend before he makes such a hasty departure," Julia teased, kissing Tom lightly on the cheek.

"Yeah." Tom shrugged his shoulders uncomfortably. "This is Frank. He's just a hitchhiker. I don't know much about him, except that he doesn't like to get too close to women."

Julia raised an eyebrow, glancing to see Frank's reaction. He was smiling sheepishly, shuffling his feet, hands in pockets. The kid was clever, but it may have backfired. Julia was now even more intrigued.

"You don't like women?" she asked him bluntly.

Frank laughed. "I love women. I'm not gay or anything. Uh — I just don't want to be tied down. That's all. I guess it scares me, so I don't stick around for long."

Julia pinned him with her gaze for a long moment. She put on her father's psychiatrist voice. "Perhaps bondage would be useful in your situation. If only your women had restrained you, maybe you could have overcome this neurotic fear. You might have become a valued mate. As it is, it seems you are doomed to run from one woman to another all your life. What a pity." She gave him a wry smile.

Frank felt a prickling at the back of his neck. Was this some bizarre cult he had been lured into? Bondage was not his idea of a good time. Julia giggled as she noticed his apprehension. She patted his arm reassuringly and sat down on the grass. Tom couldn't wait to change the subject.

CHAPTER 18

Inquisition

Ralph was pleased after reading that Julia, or Carmen as she called her former self, had been sent away by the Romanies. Now she would have to face the harsh realities of the outside world or, even better, be forced to return to her husband where she belonged. It irked him that she had left the daughter behind. Certainly, Lord Blackney had a right to his own child. She could at least have sent the baby to him without revealing her own whereabouts. But she was vengeful and wicked. She would never give the poor guy anything, not unless she was crushed into submission. Ralph hoped that would happen soon. And perhaps it would.

When he had left off at the gift of the black horse, Ralph felt a sense of evil overshadowing the tale. It seemed as if that horse was enchanted and all the infamy of the godless Gypsies would follow Carmen as long as the horse was hers. It was not a good omen.

How coincidental it all seemed to Ralph, the way Julia had run away from him just like Carmen had run from Lord Blackney. Was Julia reenacting the drama somehow? Had she gone off in search of Romanies or maybe Native Americans who lived close to nature? From the way she wrote, that would appear to be her concept of the ideal way of life. It wouldn't be the city that drew her. Not now. She had written too much about the raw, wild edges of life, the call of nature. But how could he know for sure? Her diary was his only clue. He opened the little volume and picked up where he left off.

I rode for two days before I came to a town. My tears never had time to dry. Everything I loved in my life had been left behind in one moment, my daughter, Melita, Leo, and a whole way of life to which I could never return. Sloe was my one comfort. Her large, gentle eyes seemed to read my grief as she nuzzled me with her velvet nose. She was an unusual horse, so attuned to my wishes that I barely had to guide her as I rode.

It seemed that after a while I could understand her as well. We stopped when she was tired. I listened when she pricked up her ears. When she snorted apprehensively I watched for danger and avoided being attacked by the many bandits and highwaymen who lurked along my way. By the time we reached the town I felt as if we were an inseparable team. I depended on her as if she were the best friend I would ever have. And perhaps she was. Every moment I thanked Leo for his gift. I was sure he knew much better than I what a fine creature he had parted with.

I began to practice the only trade I knew, telling fortunes, reading palms. People were wary at first, but soon they came to ask about their futures. The young witch with the black horse was a great source of entertainment for the peasantry and nobility alike. Before long I was something of a conversation piece throughout the area. I stayed in each town for a week, then moved on to another.

It was easy to collect enough silver to pay for food and lodging. My life was comfortable, but often lonely. I thought it was amusing to be called a witch, since I knew little of the craft or the religion of witches. I simply had the seeing eye, and that both frightened and fascinated the naive country folk. But there were forces moving in the world that were not

so benign. If I could have used my gift for myself, I might
have avoided a great deal of pain. The Inquisition was at
large, spreading its tentacles of fear throughout the land.

Ralph closed the diary with some satisfaction. He had too many things to do that day to spend much time reading. A cruel smile crossed his face at the mention of the Inquisition. If anything could bring her to justice, the Inquisition would. Stupid Carmen, the little slut, thinking that she could get away with her witchcraft in a Christian land.

"'Suffer not a witch to live,' Exodus 22:18," he muttered to himself as he tossed the diary aside and began to dress for church. It was Sunday morning and he only had ten minutes to get ready for Mass. Just enough time to shave and put on his suit and tie.

Julia had refused to go to Mass in the last year before she disappeared, saying that the church was an outdated and hypocritical institution. Its history was full of barbaric acts and mistreatment of women. Even now, women were treated like inferior citizens and not allowed into the priesthood. She didn't trust it and she wasn't going to have any part of it.

She had even told him that the verse from Exodus 22:18 was a mistranslation, probably intentional. And it should really say, "Suffer not a poisoner to live" — as if she was some sort of language expert. Then she went on to claim that no matter what the translation meant, nobody has a right to kill another person. It says so right in the Ten Commandments. That had stumped Ralph, but it didn't change his fear of witches and their craft.

Maybe women *were* inferior, Ralph mused to himself as he began to shave. After all, the pope was infallible and he had decided that women couldn't be priests. And Jesus hadn't exactly founded the church with a bunch of women. He chose twelve men. He must have had his reasons. Even Buddha had been wary of letting women into his religion and nobody ever said he wasn't wise. These guys know what they are doing when they start a religion. That's why people follow them, Ralph mused. Julia thinks she's wiser than Jesus or Buddha, but you don't see people following her.

Ralph's blood pressure was rising again. He was so agitated that he cut his chin with the razor and had to stop the blood with a wad of toilet paper. What really peeved him, now that he thought about it, was the time Julia told him that she didn't think Jesus ever intended to set up a church, certainly not anything like the Catholic Church.

"Then why the hell would Jesus go through the crucifixion?" Ralph had hollered at her. "He was God and could have stopped it easily."

"We are all gods," Julia had answered. "Even Jesus said that. But people go through horrible things every day without stopping them."

"Those people are not Jesus! They aren't raising the dead or turning water into wine." Ralph had countered, his temples pulsing with anger.

The girl was exasperating. Ralph had even paid quite a bit of money for her to attend Catholic school. What a waste! He had invited priests over for dinner at least once a month, made sure Julia received the sacraments and avoided missing Mass on holy days of obligation, at least until she refused outright. He had done all the right things, but none of it seemed to make a difference.

Reading Julia's diary shed some light on the problem, though. She apparently had this delusion about living with Gypsies and screwing in the woods. It was all so uncivilized and downright immoral. Utter nonsense, of course, but she seemed to believe it. Sometimes she had even sucked Ralph into her illusion as he read her words.

Maybe she really was a witch. He could almost believe that she had lived another life. The thought made him shiver with revulsion. But it also made him wonder enough that he had to ask Father McFarland at his local parish about the possibility of reincarnation. The priest told him that the church didn't take an official position against it. That surprised Ralph.

He then began to ponder the idea that her story might possibly be true. That in itself was an unnerving thought. But his greater horror was the thought that, if she had lived before, then he might have as well. And who might he have been? He didn't want to know!

CHAPTER 19

Sparks

F rank lounged on the mossy bank of the creek, down the hill from where Tom had parked his truck, watching silver ripples swirl downstream. He liked it here. This girl had found herself a haven from the welter of human chaos. His impulse to run had been matched just as quickly by an impulse to stick around, just long enough to get a better sense of who she was.

She looked about eighteen, twenty at most. Perhaps too young for his thirty-two years, but there was something old in her eyes. Mostly, he was intrigued by the way she confronted him. No woman had ever bothered to chase him down. They all let him go when he ran. This one had to know why. He smiled. She was one he would like to match wits with.

Tom and Julia had wandered down the creek a few yards. There was an awkward silence hanging between them, born of plans and hopes that had abruptly collapsed in the presence of Frank. Everything felt different now and they could not find a way to resolve the tension. This morning they had each resolved to let down the walls that stood between them. Both had decided they were ready to explore a deeper relationship, but now the moment had passed and neither of them knew how to get back to it. It felt as if something had broken.

The uneasy silence spoke more than words could say. With a sigh Julia turned to face Tom. Their eyes met with an understanding so deep and tragic that they never questioned it. Whatever had changed was irreversible. They could never go back to the way things used to be.

Tom took her in his arms and kissed her softly on the cheek. There was nothing he could say, nothing to do. His eyes stung with tears for whatever had died. He still wasn't sure what it was. Julia was still here, but more distant than ever. For a moment he felt as if she was enveloped in flames and he was helpless to rescue her. He looked at her oddly. She always seemed to know what he was thinking. He had lost her even as she was standing in front of him, but what flames had taken her away?

"It's OK, Tom," Julia squeezed his hand. "I'll always love you. You are like my brother."

Flames of passion never ask permission to enter. They barge in like demons, devouring souls. They rage like wildfire, consuming everything they touch, never giving their victims time to think. Tom was not wrong in his vision of flames, for Julia was ablaze as if her body had been cast into a furnace.

One touch of her hand against the skin of Frank's arm had told her everything she wanted to know, for the heart reads skin like a book. A single touch carries messages so complex that no mind can ever understand them. The moment her eyes looked into those of Frank Davis a spark of recognition was kindled. When her fingers grazed his arm a whole new reality dawned. She had known him before and she had loved him passionately.

The recent past, the confused yearning she had felt for Tom, seemed suddenly childish in comparison with the clarity of her attraction to Frank. It was electric and completely irrational. She felt sad for Tom. He looked so baffled, so resigned. He didn't even know what the change was all about yet, but he felt it and accepted it. He had no other choice.

After they talked about things at home and things here in the woods, Julia and Tom began to head back toward Frank. Tom supposed he wouldn't be coming to see her quite as often anymore. It wouldn't feel like such a driving need. He looked at her gravely, seeing the distracted intensity in her eyes. Before, it had always included him, even if she had never let him get very close. Now she hardly even seemed to see him.

"Were you thinking of coming home?" he asked without emotion, remembering that she had brought her backpack and sleeping bag to their meeting place.

Julia shrugged. "I'd thought about it, but I'm not quite ready yet."

"Suit yourself." Tom shrugged as he spotted Frank. He looked back at Julia. "Drop me a note if you decide to come home. I'll pick you up."

Frank got to his feet as he heard them approaching. It was easy to see that their little talk had not cleared the air.

"I guess we'll be going," Tom grumbled, glancing at Frank. "You 'bout ready?"

Frank glanced at Julia, instantaneous communication flashing between them. Then he turned to Tom. "I think I'll stay for a bit and explore the area. I kinda like it here."

Tom's eyes widened as he turned to face the woman he had desired so ardently. "Do you want him to stay?"

She shook her head and shrugged, trying to soften the blow. "It's public land. He can do what he wants."

"You didn't answer my question," Tom's voice was tight.

Julia met his gaze in silence, but he read the apology in her eyes.

Tom glared at her, suddenly aware of a churning in his gut. Without another word he spun away and dashed off through the woods toward his truck. All he could think of was getting out of there as fast as he could make that machine run. She wanted that lousy hitchhiker. Damn her! After all he had done for her and all the time he had waited. His handsome face was twisted in a mask of pain. Nothing could ease it but speed.

He climbed into the truck and turned the key violently, screeching onto the road the moment the engine turned over. Mud splattered his windshield as he bounced through puddles. He drove blindly. Faster and faster, feeling as though he was driving into a fiery pit.

He could see the flames, licking, dancing around Julia's face — though it was a dark face with flashing black eyes. And suddenly he knew. He had started that fire. He had murdered her. A horror of guilt seized him as he watched her face writhe in terror and pain, her anguished eyes entreating him for mercy. Tom slammed on the gas, crushing his eyes shut against the vision, but it didn't help.

He stood helpless in his executioner's hood, fixating on her face until the weight of his remorse overwhelmed him. With a resounding roar of desperation he leapt full length into the fire, perhaps the fire of his own guilt, clutching for the searing flesh of a woman he had never really known, but would never forget.

In that instant his truck plunged out of control down a steep precipice, smashing through trees and bursting into flames at the bottom of a gully — and at last peace filled his soul.

For a moment Julia stood listening to the angry roar of Tom's engine as he sped away. He wouldn't be back. She felt sad, but it had to be. It wasn't that she didn't love him. She just knew that it wasn't enough, could never be enough. She loved him like a brother. He had to see that too. Whatever had drawn them to each other could never be a romantic sort of love. When he touched her there was no response of her soul that ached to open itself to him. It was all too intellectual, too familiar.

With a sad smile, she glanced at Frank as the distant sound of Tom's truck faded away. She hoped Tom wouldn't be angry for long. She still wanted to be his friend. How could she have predicted that everything would suddenly feel so different? It seemed as though she had stepped from one world into another in an instant, as if her world had all been black and white, and now it was alive with color.

Frank was leaning against a tree, watching her as he rolled a long pine needle between his teeth. A glow warmed his deep-set eyes and he smiled awkwardly. Pulling the pine needle from his mouth, he tossed it aside and took a step toward Julia.

"Sorry if I messed things up with your friend there. I hoped he wouldn't take it so hard." His eyes pierced into hers. "You did want me to stay, didn't you?"

"Yeah. I was curious about you, and I'm sure we knew each other before, a long time ago. I want to catch up," she answered coyly, the amber flashing in her eyes.

"Pretty eyes." He touched her chin with one finger. No matter that he had sworn off women. She excited the male in him.

Julia turned away, conscious of the pounding in her breast. This man could sweep her off her feet if she wasn't careful. He had the power she had always hoped to find in Tom. She couldn't define it. Something animal-like, yet cultivated to a gentleness that made her want to melt against him. It was a dangerous power. One she might never be able to break away from. But then she might never want to break away. With a tiny smile she glanced back at Frank hesitantly. He was eyeing her with curiosity. Then he smiled, too.

With tender fingers he traced the line of her jaw until again he touched her chin. He pulled her face toward his with a firm, gentle pressure that melted her resistance. Julia gazed meekly into his eyes, malleable as clay in his hands. Her hesitancy vanished as he softly caressed the curve of her cheek and kissed the freckles on her nose. His breath on her face was like the warmth of sunshine, almost too exquisite to bear.

"Is this why you wanted me to stay, little Julia?" With a playful smile he pulled away from her. "Did you long for my caress?" His voice was soft and teasing.

She blushed, for she couldn't deny it. Much as she wanted to hold him back, make him beg to touch her and assert the only power she felt was left to her, she wanted his touch more. That was all Frank needed to know. With an authority that surprised her, he claimed her lips with his own, sending raw searing passion through her bones. She responded quite by instinct, never having been kissed like that before, at least not in her present life. Though she still remembered passionate kisses with Leo so very long ago in another reality.

As for Frank, there had never been a woman who could make him lose control. He was barely holding on with this one, determined not to let her overwhelm him. There was something maddeningly attractive about her, the way her hair streamed out on the breeze in wild flames about her face as if it had a life of its own, and that amber glow in her eyes. She wasn't especially beautiful, not in the ordinary sense of the word. Her presence was more majestic than anything else he could call it.

She had a magnetism like nobody he had ever met and it made him want to bend her to him and make her moan with desire. He could take her right now if he chose to. She was so ripe for it, but he didn't dare. Right now she might eat him alive and leave nothing but the bones. If she was older, more experienced, she might have sensed that and taken the opportunity to hook him, but she was young. Maybe even a virgin. That was a heady thought.

If no man had ever claimed her before, if he was the first, he would have an advantage. She wouldn't be able to compare him with anyone else, and that gave him a feeling of freedom. He could do anything and it would become for her the standard by which all others would be judged. What better way to claim a woman's heart? He kissed her fervently then, as though she was his already, and she folded softly into his arms.

Suddenly Julia jerked free, pushing Frank away, her eyes bursting in an agony of tears.

"TOM!" Her voice screeched, shaking the sky with the intensity of her pain.

Frank reeled back, staring at her as if she had gone mad. "What the hell?"

With a convulsive shudder, Julia crumpled to the ground. "Why didn't I see it? I could have warned him. I could have saved him — but he wouldn't have listened." She lay sobbing on the damp brown grass.

Frank was mystified. Why would she feel so guilty all of a sudden for sending Tom away? It didn't make sense. He could understand why she might have qualms, but this was so extreme, so abrupt. He let her cry a minute then tried to console her. "What is it, Julia?"

"He's dead!" She trembled, looking up at him helplessly, her eyes red and teary.

Something in the way she said it made Frank sure she knew. The same thing had happened to him when his brother was killed. He remembered waking up screaming Jerry's name in the middle of the night, absolutely positive that he had died. Sure enough, they received the military visit the next morning, verifying it. Such an eerie feeling.

"My God! I'm so sorry. I feel really rotten." Frank frowned, suddenly feeling the burden of guilt. "It's my fault. I should have gone with him."

"No, it was my fault. I wanted you to stay. I think I broke his heart. I only wish I had seen it before it was too late."

Convulsive sobbing overtook her again and she looked up to the sky, shaking in her agony. Then a strange glow came over her face. Frank was far away. Her eyes softened as an indescribable rapture spread through her, pouring out from her heart and tingling through her body like a shower of light.

She whispered Tom's name fervently, like a prayer, basking in blissful communion with his soul. All her longing was concentrated into this one moment and satisfied. Like Wagner's Isolde rejoicing in transcendent love with her slain Tristan, Julia swooned in supreme ecstasy. An ecstasy that pierced the veil of death. Her face was transformed in that moment, radiant with the beauty of all-encompassing love.

Frank was not a stupid man. He watched in awe as she so surely entered a blissful state of love that surpassed all mere physical pleasure. It was clear now that he would never be the first, nor even the last man to claim the love of Julia Flynn. All he knew was that he had to be in there somewhere.

He was captive to this strangely lovely woman who communed with spirits as freely as she did with the living. His lovemaking could only be anticlimactic, mundane, after the mystical rapture he was witnessing now. No mortal man could bring her to the heights she had found with her dying Tom. At least, he was certain he never could.

CHAPTER 20

Intrusion

⊙⊙

Tom's accident was reported in all the North-state newspapers, with a photo of his truck, charred and smashed, being hauled up the steep cliff. A recent high school graduation picture was included, along with a brief summary of Tom's life and mention of his surviving family members. The possibility of foul play made it a newsworthy story, though there were no suspects. It just seemed very odd that he was found burned to death more than two hundred miles from home.

Nobody seemed to know why Tom had been driving up north that day. He had been expected to show up at work by five o'clock that evening. It made no sense. Yet, while it seemed unlikely that he would drive up there on a whim, the suspicion of kidnapping or murder seemed even more remote. It would probably remain a mystery.

Ralph had saved the clippings from several newspapers. He now kept them folded between the pages of Julia's diary. It seemed fitting. Only three days after Tom's accident, he had found the diary and begun to read it. Slowly, he was putting the pieces of the puzzle together.

He picked up her diary once again and pulled out a clipping with Tom's photo. For a long time he sat reminiscing about the tall, handsome kid who had played such a big part in Julia's life. He wondered if she knew he was dead. There was an inkling in his bones that she knew far more about it than anyone else. It was a strange feeling, almost like a premonition. Or, he thought with a jolt, maybe Tom had gone to see Julia and found her dead somewhere. That could have caused him to drive off the road in his despair.

It was a chilling thought. But Ralph couldn't bring himself to believe that Julia was dead. He couldn't accept that, no matter how annoying her ideas might be. He flipped through the pages of the diary until a passage about Tom caught his eye, as if by coincidence.

Things are really starting to come together in my mind. I remember who Tom was in my past life and I have forgiven him for burning me at the stake. He didn't do it with malice. Also, I have recognized that my grandmother, Carol, was my father in that same lifetime. That sounds weird, but it makes so much sense now that I think about it. He was such a domineering, thoughtless man who had little concern for my feelings. I was no more than a dog to him. In fact, I think he was more considerate of his hunting dogs than he ever was of his daughter.

I suppose that's just the way men were in those days. Women had so little power over their own lives that men simply treated them as possessions, or even burdens. I'm sure it was a great relief to my father when Lord Blackney took me off his hands.

Maybe that accounts for the strong feelings I have always had about my grandmother. She doesn't know it, but I have felt a mixture of attachment and wariness toward her, as though I couldn't really trust her to be there when I needed her. The reason she wanted to take me in after my parents died was probably so that she could make amends and balance the karma, even if she wasn't conscious of it. I wouldn't have refused her, except that I had another direction to explore at the time — one that I am beginning to regret. But I suppose it had to be.

Ralph closed the diary and leaned back in his chair. That last line made him wonder. Could she be talking about him? But he was too preoccupied with the accident to follow that thought. He felt sure that Tom had known where Julia was hiding and that his untimely death was somehow connected with her. As he mused over his suspicions, he became more and more certain that he was on the right track. Finally, he decided he would drive up to the site of the accident and take a look around.

Tom couldn't have gone far from where he had met Julia, Ralph deduced, since it was still early afternoon when the accident occurred. The boy had been working at his restaurant job the night before, so he must have driven up that morning. The accident happened on a road through the national forest and Tom's truck appeared to have been heading back toward home. Ralph guessed that Julia would be within five or ten miles of the accident site.

He climbed into his Honda Civic and headed north, with a well-worn CD of jazz classics blaring at top volume. If he was going to spend half his weekend driving, he may as well have his favorite music to ease the monotony. He sped through familiar suburbs and then out to the open countryside beyond, propelled by a zeal that bordered on fanatical. The hours seemed to rush by. Once he reached the national forest, Ralph had an easy time finding the accident site. The papers had described it so thoroughly that it almost jumped out at him as he drove slowly up the road.

Broken trees and crushed undergrowth on the roadside gave the spot away. Good thing it had recently rained, Ralph mused, or there would have been one hell of a forest fire. He parked and climbed down to where the truck had landed and fire had blackened the hillside. It gave him an eerie feeling to think that Tom had perished there in flames. Reality wavered as he stood gazing at the scorched earth and for a moment he felt as if he was looking for bones in the ashes. A strange sense of déjà vu ran through him, but he shook it off as he headed back up the hill to his car.

If he figured right, Julia would be somewhere to the north. Why not take a look? Ralph started his engine and headed up the road, straining his eyes for some sign of human habitation. Naturally, Julia wouldn't camp near the road, but perhaps there would be a path leading off, or some other sign of human presence. He explored several trails that ended in tangles of underbrush, then spotted one that ran down a steep hill and angled off into the thick of the forest.

Feeling like a hound on a scent, Ralph followed the trail down into the narrow valley and then up a rise to where he could look out over several hundred acres of forested land. There was no sign of a camp, but still, he felt like he was homing in. If only he could see through that beastly mass of trees and brush. He was certain he would find some trace of Julia.

From where he was standing he could easily find his way back to the car, but if he got into the thick of the trees he would surely lose his sense of direction. His compass gave him small comfort. A tiny compass against the vastness of the wilderness didn't inspire much confidence. Still, it was better than nothing. He checked his bearings and headed due north with his sense of mission driving him forward.

On entering the heavy growth of forest, he could barely see more than twenty yards in any direction. He plodded step after step, straining his senses for signs of life. After three hours of weaving his way from the hill into the trees and up another hill, he was beginning to feel that it was hopeless. How could he ever find one girl in the middle of this tangle of vegetation? He turned back toward his car, feeling foolish for ever imagining he would have any luck.

Damn that girl anyway! After all the trouble she had given him, he should just let her go, but for some reason he couldn't. He had developed a possessive attachment to Julia, having been proud of her achievements and vicariously pleased with her schoolgirl triumphs. Besides, she had chosen to live with him of her own free will. That meant something. Nobody else had ever done that. Now that she was gone, it felt like a vacuum was sucking at his soul. A void yawned open and only Julia could fill it.

He pushed his way angrily through the brush, finally breaking into a clearing on a hill. From there he could see a wooded area where the trees grew more sparsely. The thick firs and pines gave way to oak and bay. He blinked his eyes and rubbed them for, as often happens with those who have given up hope, he now had reason to believe his luck was changing. It seemed as if he saw a wisp of smoke off to the east, not too far from where he was standing. It might have been mist rising from a warm spring, or even his imagination, but as he stared at it he became convinced that it was indeed smoke.

With rising excitement he checked his compass and set off to explore this new phenomenon. It took him another hour, heading through light brush, to reach the outskirts of the clearing from which the smoke arose. Then he was caught by surprise. A man sat beside the fire, quietly whittling a chunk of pine. Behind him was a tiny hut.

"I'll be damned!" His voice broke the silence.

The whittler jerked to his feet and gasped in surprise. "Who the hell are you?"

Frank had been so absorbed in his thoughts that the racket of Ralph's approach had only made a dull impression on him. He had imagined it was just a large deer or perhaps Julia returning to the camp. Now he stood with his knife raised, mouth agape and adrenaline pumping, ready to defend his territory.

"Hold on there," Ralph answered with some apprehension. He held up his open palms. "I'm unarmed. Can I just ask you a couple of questions?"

Frank shrugged. "Sorry. You scared the shit outa me." He heaved a sigh.

"You live out here?" Ralph began to relax as he nodded toward the hut.

"For the moment." Frank returned to his stump stool. "Why don't you have a seat? You look exhausted." He gestured toward a log by the fire, then picked up his whittling and resumed where he had left off.

"I'm looking for someone," Ralph stated, still standing. "Maybe you've seen her. A red-haired girl named Julia. I have reason to believe that she came up here a few months ago."

Frank's jaw tensed, but he kept his expression carefully neutral. "Can't imagine a girl surviving out here for long. This is rough country. You know, bears, cougars. She's probably moved on to someplace a little more civilized." He was thinking to himself how strangely coincidental it was that Julia had just left that morning to visit her grandmother.

"So you haven't seen her." Ralph felt his hopes sinking.

"I can't say as I have. Though," Frank's eyes were twinkling with mischief now, "the Indians have a tale about a red demon who runs naked through the woods, wailing like a woman. Does that sound like your friend?"

To Frank's surprise, Ralph perked up at this news. "Where would I find them, these Indians? Do they live in these woods?"

"I don't think so. I expect they only come here for recreation or hunting, but there's a reservation not far from here. I'm guessing that's where they live. You'd have to find it on a map."

"Really," Ralph mused. "Do you know the name of the tribe or anything? I'd like to check it out. Julia is all I have in the world. I have to find her."

"You know, I don't think they ever gave me any names. I think they only told me the red demon story to scare me off. Kinda makes me curious though. Anything that wails like a woman sounds like fair game to me." He winked at Ralph with a man-to-man grin.

Ralph raised a rusty eyebrow, suspiciously observing his host. At the same time he noticed that the light was beginning to fade. It faded fast in the woods, the lingering twilight cut off by the deep shadows of the trees. He would never make it back to his car before dark.

Frank glanced up at the sky. "You'd better head back if you want to get to the road before nightfall. I'd say you have just enough time if you leave now."

"I'll never make it," Ralph argued. "It took me hours to get this far."

"You went the hard way," Frank laughed. "There's a trail that'll get you out there in half an hour, but suit yourself. You're welcome to stretch out here by the fire for the night if you want. I've got a spare sleeping bag." He shrugged as if it didn't matter to him one way or the other. "By the way, my name's Frank. I guess I haven't been very hospitable." He stood up, extending his hand.

"Ralph McCullen." As they shook hands Ralph made up his mind.

"Yeah, I think I will stay the night if you don't mind. I'd like to look around a little more in the morning."

He huddled close to the fire, pulling off his daypack and setting it on the ground beside him with an exaggerated sigh. Then he dug out a bottle of water and some beef jerky.

"Help yourself," he motioned to Frank as he prepared to eat.

Frank glanced at him curiously and declined his offer. He hadn't been able to eat meat for over a decade. "Who is this Julia to you, anyway? Are you a relative?"

"She's my niece," Ralph answered simply, relieved to be able to talk about her. "She disappeared a few months ago and the police never found a trace of her. I always suspected that she ran off to hide somewhere in the wilderness. I don't know why.

"I didn't think too much about it until I saw in the paper that her boyfriend was killed in an auto accident somewhere up here. Not far from this spot, actually." He cocked his head in the direction of the road. "That got me wondering again. Why would Tom have driven all the way up here by himself, if it wasn't to see Julia? So I followed his trail. I think it will lead me to her sooner or later."

Ralph went on talking without noticing the paleness that had crept over Frank's face. He was doing his best not to reveal his emotions, but the words "boyfriend" and "killed" had sent a chill of remorse through him. It sounded like Tom had a long history with Julia. This guy was calling him her boyfriend. And in the end the kid had been rejected for another man — a complete stranger at that. No wonder he drove himself off a cliff.

Frank and Julia had hiked out to the accident site and left an offering of bread and wildflowers in the ashes to appease the disturbed spirits of the place. He still had a clear picture of it in his mind. It was hard to shake his feeling of guilt. He had known that Tom was interested in Julia, but that didn't count for much in his book. Tom could have courted her for years without being able to win her. Heck, Frank was interested too, but he would never take a woman away from a man once she had made her choice. That would just invite complications and drama.

"So her boyfriend was killed, huh?" Frank asked cautiously. "How did it happen?"

Ralph gave him a penetrating glance. "He drove off a cliff. Probably took a turn too fast, or hit a patch of ice. They found his truck smashed and burned. His body was charred beyond recognition. They had to identify him with dental records. Something told me it had a connection with Julia, so I came up here to investigate."

"The poor guy probably never knew what hit him." Frank shook his head and sat absorbed in thought for a long while.

By this time it was getting dark and cold. Frank went into the hut and came back with a sleeping bag that he handed to his guest. Ralph quickly unrolled it and crawled inside. Bunching up his jacket as a pillow, he laid his head down and gazed into the fire. It wasn't long before he was sound asleep. Frank whittled as the dark closed in around him. There was something about this intruder that made him nervous.

In the morning, Ralph spent several hours searching the area, then gave up. He hadn't found any trace of Julia, though a strange chill had come over him when he looked into Frank's hut. It was nothing he could put his finger on. Just a familiar feeling. Perhaps it reminded him of his niece, but he couldn't say why.

The walls were neatly lined with baskets. There was a cot along one side and a crude, stone fireplace built into the opposite wall. It could have been anybody's place, but it didn't seem to be Frank's style. He didn't strike Ralph as the kind of guy who would decorate the walls with pretty feathers and dried flowers.

In fact, the little that was there reflected a sensitive and feminine taste that contrasted sharply with the rugged persona of his host. But Ralph was too preoccupied with the passing of time to take much notice of his misgivings. He turned away and quickly gathered up his few belongings, preparing to leave.

Something caught his eye as he glanced at the hut one last time. Carved into the wood on the outside of the door was a hex symbol such as he had seen painted on barns in New England, presumably to keep evil spirits away. They had always given him the creeps.

He associated them with witchcraft, an evil he had dreaded since childhood with amazing tenacity. His dread had no basis in experience, but it had haunted even his earliest memories. Now the familiar childhood terror clutched at his heart and he hastened to make his departure. Whether Frank was a proponent of witchcraft or not didn't interest Ralph. It was bad enough that he was living in such proximity with that symbol of evil.

CHAPTER 21

Grandma

As Carol McCullen eyed her reflection in the mirror, she wondered how she could have gathered so much extra skin with age. Everything else seemed to diminish, but skin had a way of expanding to hang in folds and wrinkles on every surface of her body. She could understand it if she had been losing weight. Then, of course the skin would sag over the places where fat had filled it out before, but she was heavier now than she had ever been in all her sixty-seven years. Not really overweight, but maturely thickened about the middle. She couldn't prevent it anymore, no matter how many diets and exercise regimes she forced herself through.

But she was still good looking. At her age you either were or you weren't. There was no middle ground, no youthful bloom to fool the eye of the beholder. She had taken great care to stay on the good side of her mirror, with facials once a week along with her regular hair appointment and careful control of her diet. It showed now. Even in her late sixties she was one of the most well-preserved women of her generation. Strangers often took her for a woman ten or fifteen years younger. That gave her great satisfaction.

Decorating was another satisfaction of hers. Whether it was a person or a room, or even a whole building, Carol could lose herself in the possibilities for bringing out its very best qualities. For years she had done it professionally, after her husband, Pete, died. Julia was about seven then, so it must have been almost twelve years ago now. Carol tried not to think about it too much. The years had just rolled by, pulling her along with them. Without Pete, life had never seemed as meaningful. His death had made her a sadder and a deeper person. Family ties that hadn't seemed so important suddenly felt vital.

Only six years later her daughter, Missy, was killed in the plane crash. Now all she had left was Ralph — and Julia, but nobody knew what had happened to her. She had simply disappeared. Carol had loved to dress that girl in fancy outfits when she was little, but then Ralph had stolen her away.

It wasn't Julia's fault. The child didn't realize how much her grandmother was hurt by her rejection. She had to make her own choices and for some reason it suited her to live with Ralph. Carol couldn't imagine why. It seemed that the two of them had nothing in common. There was something so annoying about the whole situation that it aggravated her to think about it.

She pushed it from her mind, running a tortoise-shell comb through her still strawberry blond hair. Her hairdresser took greater and greater pains to keep it that way. Lately he was suggesting that she let it go gray. It would look more natural at her age, he said, but somehow she just didn't feel ready to look that old. She had always envied Julia her wild flame of hair. Not so light as hers, but full of bright fire tints that flashed and gleamed in the sunlight. Julia would never be able to get that from a bottle.

Pleased with her reflection at last, Carol padded out to the kitchen in her fluffy pink slippers. Bosco howled outside the kitchen door and she rushed to open it for him.

"Poor little puppy," she purred, picking up the drenched pug as he scampered under her feet. Mommy forgot it was raining outside."

She ran to get her blow dryer and aimed it at the soggy and shivering little dog. Bosco's bulging eyes watered in the heat of the dryer, but he seemed to appreciate the warmth. Soon he rolled himself up in his bed with a contented grunt and Carol set about making herself breakfast.

Julia was on her mind this morning. She had dreamed about her last night.

That tragedy with her friend, Tom, had been such a shock. Carol had seen it in the newspaper last week and it brought back so many memories of Julia. Young people these days seem to live on the edge of tragedy. Drugs and shootings and suicide were on the rise. She took a loaf of bread from the freezer and popped two slices into the toaster.

A knock at the kitchen door jolted her out of her reverie. Who in the world would have come around to the back door? Carol made an annoyed face. She had hoped to have a day to herself for a change, but obviously she was in such demand that it would probably never happen. It made her feel important, but sometimes it also felt like a burden. She made her way to the door and pulled it open. Her heart skipped a beat when she discovered her granddaughter, dirty and bedraggled, but essentially well, standing on her back stoop.

"Hi Grandma," Julia greeted her casually. Then, after an awkward pause, "Can I come in?"

Carol stood frozen in the doorway. With great effort she stepped back and let Julia pass through. Bosco had been barking frantically and she finally gathered her senses enough to tell him to shut up. Julia grinned.

"Hey, Bosco, don't you remember me? Come here you little varmint." He began wagging his curly stub of a tail violently, peeing all over the floor as he wiggled his way toward her. Julia looked apologetically at her grandmother. "Sorry, I got him a little over-excited."

She grabbed a handful of paper towels and began to wipe up the dog pee from the linoleum. "He sure has a big bladder for the size of him," Julia laughed as she dropped the soggy towels in the trash and went to the sink to wash her hands.

'That he does," Carol almost laughed, beginning to regain her composure. "But Julia! Where on earth have you been?" Her arms flew around the girl. "I've been worried sick about you."

Julia gave a sigh as she answered, still hugging her grandmother. "It's a long story. The short answer is that I've been camping. I had a sort of breakdown, but I'm fine now. I didn't mean to upset you. I — I just had to get away."

Carol pulled back. "Breakdown? Why didn't you call me to ask for help, or at least let us know you were all right? Your uncle and I have been going through hell with worry."

"I'm sorry. I really didn't want to see Uncle Ralph. I couldn't. I was afraid I would —," she broke off abruptly.

"What?" Carol's voice was softer now. "You were afraid of what?"

"I can't talk about it now." Julia was shivering.

"Okay, it can wait." Carol stroked Julia's hair. "I'm just glad you're back home, safe and sound. Let's find you some dry clothes."

"Did you hear about Tom?" The girl asked suddenly, peering intently at Carol as she pulled a long white bathrobe from the dryer and offered it to Julia.

"Yes, honey. I saw it in the paper. I'm so sorry. I know he was a good friend of yours."

"He had just left me when it happened. I feel so guilty about it." She wiped a tear from her cheek. "He was really upset with me. I heard him drive away and then I just knew." Her voice was trailing off. "He was burned to death."

"He was a good boy. I'm sure he went straight to heaven," Carol stated reassuringly.

"Oh come on Grandma! You know I don't believe in all that." Julia spoke with annoyance. Then her voice softened. "Well, I know he found peace, anyway. I could feel that when he passed on. I suppose you could call that heaven, at least while it lasts."

Carol gave her an odd look, but didn't pursue the issue. She pulled her now-cold toast out of the toaster and asked casually, "Does your uncle know you're home?"

Julia stiffened. "No! And I don't want him to know."

"Oh? You've had a falling out?"

"What's to fall out from? He's in his own little world and I'm in mine." Julia looked at Carol with a twinge of fear. "You won't tell him I was here, will you? I'm not ready to face him yet."

"Your secret is safe with me, dear. I never understood why you chose to live with him in the first place." She hoped the pained tone in her voice was not too obvious. "So, what now?"

"Well, I was hoping I could stay with you for a little while — just until I find a job and my own place. It wouldn't be for too long."

"Of course! You are always welcome here, Julia. You know I've wanted that ever since your parents died. I still have that room fixed up for you down the hall."

Julia grinned. "You mean the one with the pink canopy bed and dust ruffle?"

"Well, you were younger then. You were my little princess," Carol smiled weakly as she eyed Julia's tanned skin. "I guess you'll want to make it more rustic now. How about a safari theme?"

"It's fine, Grandma. I'm very adaptable." Julia chuckled. Carol was strangely quiet. She cleared her throat before asking the question that had been burning in her heart for years. "Julia, why did you choose to stay with Ralph? I thought it was because you didn't like me."

"Grandma!" Julia was exasperated. "I was afraid you would think that, but I knew you wouldn't listen if I told you any different. It had nothing to do with you. It was about Uncle Ralph. I needed to remember something about him. That's all I can tell you."

"All right, I won't pry. But, could you tell me one more thing?"

"What?" Julia looked at her grandmother with a wary frown.

"The lawyer," Carol eyed her seriously. "What did you tell him that scared him away so quickly when I was trying to get custody?"

Julia laughed out loud. "That's easy. I told him I knew what I was doing and that he should stay out of it." Her eyes sparkled impishly. "Plus, I mentioned certain indiscretions of his and asked if he would like me to share them with his wife. He was totally shocked that I knew things about him that no one else knew. I basically scared him into doing what I wanted." She laughed again. "That took care of him. I'm sorry if it was rough on you. I never meant to hurt you."

Though, Julia thought to herself, there was a certain poetic justice in it. When her grandmother had been Carmen's father, she had not valued her family members much. This time around she had learned the hard way that family was the most important thing in her life. The loss of her husband and her only daughter had hit her hard. Now Ralph and Julia were all she had left, and even Julia had vanished for a time. Through it all, Carol had learned to care very deeply.

She had also learned the value of womanhood. A forced marriage was as repugnant to her now as it had been acceptable to her as Carmen's father. In her present life, she was adamant about women's rights. Carol had made it very clear to her husband, Pete, right from the start that he had better treat her as an equal or he could get lost.

She needn't have bothered trying to convince Pete. He had adored her from the moment they met. He knew that Carol could easily match him on any level. Back then she was stunning in her beauty and powerful in her presence. He was almost in awe of her. She was just as awestruck with him and that made it a perfect match. They had lived together like a pair of lovebirds until the day he died.

Julia sat in a kitchen chair scratching Bosco under the chin. She looked up, feeling her grandmother's eyes on her. Carol had almost answered that it had hurt when Julia rejected her, intended or not, but something made her stop. She watched Julia intently, a small frown on her well-preserved brow, and shook her head.

"You know, Julia, sometimes I think you're just like your mother, so wild and uninhibited. I never understood her either, but I didn't love her any less for it."

Carol was feeling strangely exposed, but she couldn't find a reason for the feeling. In the heart of it she felt at peace, as though a new understanding had come between herself and her granddaughter. The clouds had cleared between them. They could be friends.

CHAPTER 22

Dawn

The hours passed slowly for Frank after his surprise visitor left. Unsettled thoughts churned through his mind as he cooked himself a late lunch over the fire. Canned beans, garlic and onions filled the air with a mouthwatering aroma, but his mind was far away. He was curious about Julia and Ralph, wondering what sort of relationship they shared.

It seemed to him that her uncle was keeping way too much information to himself. After all, Julia had run off to live in the woods without even letting him know she was alive. That told him a lot. There must be a good reason why she didn't want the guy to find her. Perhaps he had molested her. He had that kind of lecherous vibe.

By nightfall Frank was weary and agitated. He wondered if he should try to warn Julia that her uncle was out looking for her. That, in fact, he had come very close to finding her. It was only a lucky coincidence that she was off visiting her grandmother when Ralph showed up. Frank could tell that Ralph was suspicious, though. He might be back.

About half an hour before dawn Frank awoke with a start. Something had rattled his sleep. Perhaps it was only a dream, but his blood rushed furiously, pounding in his head. Was Ralph back already? The dark was still thick around him and he strained his eyes into the blackness expecting to meet another pair of eyes. Instead he saw the darting beam of a flashlight and then a smile, white teeth glistening in the dim glow.

"Julia!" He sat bolt upright.

"Hi Frank," she sighed wearily. "How's it going?"

"You scared the crap out of me, but otherwise I'm all right." He began to relax, stretching out in his sleeping bag as she sat beside him. "I didn't expect you back so soon."

"A friend of my grandmother's was heading up this way. I had to snag a ride when I could." She eyed him curiously. "You seem kind of jumpy. What's going on?"

"Well," he paused for a moment, watching her face. "There was this guy looking for you. Said he was your uncle."

Julia stiffened. "Oh shit! He actually found his way here?"

"I think it was pure luck. He wasn't much of a woodsman."

"That's putting it mildly," she snorted. "He barely leaves the house except to go to work, or church two blocks away. It's kind of scary that he could find this place. What did you tell him?"

Frank leaned his head back on his arm and looked up at the fading stars with a grin. "I said I'd been ravishing you every night and I couldn't wait until you got back so I could do it some more."

"Oh boy! That ought to make him bristle."

"Unfortunately, I didn't think of it until now," he chuckled, "but if I see him again that's what I'll tell him."

Julia laughed. Then she looked directly at Frank. "Is that what you have in mind, ravishing me every night?"

He couldn't tell if she was mocking or inviting. "I've often thought of it," he admitted, "but maybe it's not what I really want."

"I guess you got quite a shock last time you tried." She smiled, but her voice was sad. She seemed to be talking to herself.

"Yeah. Maybe that's what it is. Something happened between you and Tom that was beyond anything I've ever experienced. It kinda scared me. I mean, it was like you were off in another world."

"Well, I hope you can experience it someday with someone."

"I really feel like I screwed things up," Frank spoke quietly, after a long pause. "You probably wonder why I'm still here."

"I know why you're here." Julia stretched out on the dry grass beside him, watching the twilight dissolve the stars. "I haven't let you go yet."

Frank raised an eyebrow, but said nothing.

"I haven't let Ralph go either, but he doesn't realize it. He thinks he owns me, like a pet."

Frank laughed. "Yeah, right! You seem like the last person anybody could own."

Julia laughed with a snort. "Uncle Ralph has no idea who I am. But he thinks — or he thought he was in control of me. He thought I was playing his game, but then I slipped out of his grip. I'm sure that freaked him out. The ball is in my court now. He doesn't like that."

"But why did you leave him?" Frank broached the subject cautiously. "Did he mistreat you?"

Julia gave him a piercing look. "Ralph wouldn't dare mistreat me. He knows better. But in a past life he destroyed me, utterly. I haven't forgiven him for that."

Frank sat up with a frown. "I don't know about that reincarnation stuff. Do you actually remember living before?"

"Oh yeah! Unfortunately I do." Julia nodded emphatically. "I remember way too much about it. That's why I had to run away. I felt like I was losing my mind. I was afraid I might have killed Ralph if I had stayed any longer. I almost did kill him, but I was sleepwalking. I woke up just in time."

"Okay," Frank spoke slowly, "I can see that you're really angry with him about something in the past, but... you're saying there's nothing he's ever done to you in this life? He's a relatively normal guy now?"

"Ha! I wouldn't go that far," she snorted sarcastically. "He's a neurotic pervert. I mean, look at him."

"He is a bit odd looking, I have to agree. And he did seem kind of sleazy or something. I don't know."

"Yeah. You got it." Julia sat up and tossed a log onto the fire. "You should see the women's underwear collection he hides in a box under his bed. He likes to dress up in it. He thinks I don't know, but I see things. I know all his stupid little secrets. The computer porn. The way he likes to watch snails mating, and how he steals bras and panties from unsuspecting relatives when he goes to visit them. He probably even has some of mine. He's disgusting."

"Sounds like he's a little oversexed."

"I'll say! One time he even tried seducing one of my friends. A high school girl! It was at my last birthday party. He was a little drunk, but that's no excuse. He actually told her he wanted to lick her all over. Yuck! Can you imagine anything more disgusting? I couldn't believe it. She wouldn't even talk to me after that, but I can't really blame her. I mean, I was living with the creep!"

"That's definitely shocking behavior." Frank had to agree.

"You know," Julia continued, "what makes it even worse is that he acts like it never happened, and he's not sorry at all. I was there, just around the corner. I heard him say it, but he swears he never did. He lives in a fantasy world." Julia paused searching for words. "See, I am the only person who ever chose to live with him and that made him feel like he was fooling everyone. He imagined that I admired him. So he exaggerated his pious facade more than ever, because he thought it was working. It's so pathetic. He's like the emperor with no clothes trying to appear as everyone's ideal. But in reality he's a very screwed-up guy. His fatal flaw is that he tries to fool everyone into thinking he's perfect, but he doesn't fool anyone."

"And I suppose you're above all that?" Frank eyed her with amusement.

"You're mocking me," she pouted.

"A little. But seriously, don't you think you have a bit of a facade too."

"It's not that exaggerated. And I hope by the time I'm his age I'll be way more together than he is."

"I hope so too," Frank teased.

Julia let out a sigh. "I know I'm not perfect. I should keep my own doorstep clean and all that." She had lost the strident tone in her voice. "I guess it's easier to just be myself when I'm out here in the woods and there's nobody around to judge me. Much harder when I care what people think."

Now she was remembering just how hard it could be to stand up for the truth in the face of judgment. Not so long ago people had even been burned for it.

After a long silence, Frank spoke again. "Do you care what I think of you, Julia?"

She hesitated a moment, then answered. "Yeah, Frank, I guess I do."

As the sun streaked the sky with a rosy glow, Julia sat pondering Frank's question. Why did she care? Frank wasn't the sort of person she wanted to impress. Even so, his presence made her feel less spontaneous. When alone, she could completely be herself. With Frank there she felt just a hint of inhibition.

She hadn't come out here to be alone. She had simply run away, looking for a place to hide, thinking that the vastness of the forest could swallow her and all her rage.

Something inside of her had snapped. An uncontrollable fury had threatened to be unleashed at the slightest provocation. She had wanted to lose herself in the wild heart of nature until it healed her wounds — or killed her. At that point she hadn't cared which.

But why this particular forest? She had run away from her old life, but it also felt as if something had called her — as if this very forest had always been calling her. Or maybe it was Margaret Littlewolf, who she now recognized as Melita from her former life, the wise Romani woman who had rescued her when she ran away from Lord Blackney.

With a sense of wonder Julia slipped into a trance, remembering the feeling of that wild call, like the faraway howling of wolves. Melita-Margaret was there with her even now as her guiding spirit. Maybe she would always be there, waiting to rescue her whenever she lost her way.

Julia looked up at the mass of tree branches overhead, their rough bark glowing in stark detail as the sun began to penetrate the thick canopy of needled branches and autumn leaves. She could smell the sweet, musty scent of bay laurel leaves decomposing into mulch and she breathed it in deeply. Frank seemed as if he was made of wood, growing there like one of the trees. Did she care what he thought? His question echoed in her mind. Why did it matter? Did she care what the trees thought?

CHAPTER 23

Jean Ferrier

After his adventure in the woods, Ralph had dragged himself back to his house with weary bones and collapsed into his favorite chair in front of the television. His trip had been unfruitful. Though he didn't feel that it was a complete waste of time. There was still something eating at him about that hut. More and more he felt that Frank was out of place there. But that meant it had to be someone else's hut and there wasn't anyone else around — at least not while he was there.

It was unlikely that he could have stumbled on Julia's hideout so easily. But then again, why not? He knew her pretty well. Tom had been somewhere very close by. The little hut was probably the only dwelling within miles, so it was certainly possible that she had stayed there, at least for a while. And that Frank fellow could have been lying, perhaps to protect Julia's secret. What if he was her lover? She could have run off with him and then Tom had tracked her down and tried to win her back. Failing that, he may have been upset enough to drive off the road. That wasn't so far fetched.

With a frustrated sigh, Ralph picked up Julia's diary from the coffee table in front of him and leaned back in his chair. His curiosity was mild, but soon he became engrossed in her story once again.

I spent two years wandering through Spain before I knew for certain that the Inquisition was on my trail. Moving from

106

town to town, I never stayed anywhere for long. I called myself Isobel, after my daughter, so that my name couldn't be traced. Still, my reputation spread. I was recognized in many places by my black mare, Sloe. The monks of the Inquisition had many spies who went about sniffing out heretics, but I managed to avoid them by staying on the move.

An old Jewish man, whom I only knew as Solomon, warned me that the spies were keeping watch for me. His race was also being persecuted, as well as the Cathars and Romanies. No one was safe from the Inquisition unless they were sworn Catholics — and even they were at risk if they were women who lived alone, especially if they had land and money.

I had seen my little daughter several times since I left the Romanies. Melita brought her into the towns where I was reading palms and telling fortunes. Somehow the Romanies always seemed to know where I was by some underground communication network. It surprised me, but I was always very happy to see them.

Isobel was three years old when Melita told me they were heading for the Pyrenees Mountains. Life was too dangerous for them near the towns. They would have to keep moving to avoid the Inquisition, which meant that I might never see them or my daughter again. (Little did they know, the curse of the Inquisition would continue on for hundreds of years.)

Solomon offered to take me with him to Occitania where his family had already settled. There I would be unknown and perhaps safer. I could leave behind my trade and work with his wife in the fields. It would be a good life, but I hesitated, hoping that I could continue reading palms a little longer without being discovered. I thought I just had to keep moving. But then something happened that choked me with fear.

The name of Hugh Blackney was mentioned at an inn where I was spending the night. The innkeeper talked with two men who had come from the city. They said they were under orders from Lord Blackney to search the parish for heretics, witches and all other rabble who refused to swear allegiance to the church. It was emphasized especially that Lord Blackney, now chief of the Inquisitor's spies, was intent on locating a young woman by the name of Carmen Blackney, or perhaps Carmen de la Rosa, if she had reverted to her maiden name — his wife who had vanished after a few weeks of marriage.

The innkeeper was solemn and silent as he listened to them. He knew my craft well enough. I slipped silently out of the inn and roused Sloe from her sleep in the stable.

"We have to run, my lady," I whispered in her ear as I saddled her.

And run we did, straight to Solomon's house. He was just finishing his packing and was about to leave for good.

"Take me with you," I panted. "Lord Blackney has sent spies after me."

"They will not find you in Occitania. Blackney's power does not extend that far. But we must hurry."

We rode hard for three days, finally arriving at the home of his wife and children. They welcomed me as one of their own, though at first they were suspicious, sensing that I was of the noble class.

It might have been wise to part with my fine Romani mare at that point, but I had given up too much already. Besides, she had been my only companion for so long, it would have been like selling a friend. I couldn't bear to part with her. She ran among the farm horses like a shadow, black as night. At least she seemed content.

As for myself, I was simply glad to be safe. The farm work wore me down. I wasn't strong like the peasants who had worked the fields all their lives. But a wealthy widower in the local town soon noticed and took pity on me. His wife had died in childbirth a few months earlier, and he needed someone to cook and look after his children. He took me on, giving me room and board in exchange for such duties. He was a kind and gentle man and he made me laugh when I was sad. Often I would cry at night, wishing I could have been his wife instead of having been forced to marry the hateful Lord Blackney.

His name was Jean Ferrier and he owned lands as far as the eye could see. Sometimes he would take me out riding with him and show me the borders of his domain. His blue eyes would sparkle as he saw the awe in my face. I liked to imagine that I was his wife, riding at his side to inspect our estate.

In time, I grew to trust him, but I never spoke of my marriage or my child. That would have been dangerous, for the Inquisition had ways of extracting information even from the most unwilling informers. The less anyone knew, the better. But often Jean and I would talk together in the evening after the children were asleep. Sometimes our eyes would meet by chance and a strange current would run through me. I always looked away quickly, but not before I noticed him smiling to himself.

I would have given anything to have him put his arms around me. It had been so long since I had been loved that way, as a woman. But this man was no Romani lad. He would no more think of taking a married woman in his arms than he would think of murdering his children. Yet there was a longing between us and it grew stronger as time went on.

We each had our reasons for holding back, I because I knew he would reject me if he knew of my marriage and he because of the recent death of his wife. He still wore mourning clothes and seemed to be waiting for some prescribed length of time before he would make serious advances toward me. It was very uncomfortable, since I knew I would have to tell him the truth. Yet I could not bear to leave and I hoped that he would let me stay on even if I could not be his wife.

For nearly a year we shared the joys and trials of family life. His children were like my own and the three-year-old reminded me of my little Isobel. She was a frail thing with wide blue eyes and a bright smile, but her hair was golden, unlike Isobel's. I often held her on my lap with tears in my eyes, remembering the last time I had held my daughter.

Jean would watch me, never dreaming what misery wrenched my soul. His gentle face smiled benignly as he waited patiently for the children to go to bed. Then he would come alive, delighting me with stories about his childhood and his adventures as a young man. Sometimes he talked about his estate as if it were only a matter of time before I would share it with him. I could hardly bear it. If he hadn't been so kind I would have been able to go about my work, hardly noticing him, but the sweetness of his attentions made me grow to love him.

The spring of the year brought a heightened passion to our longing and one day, after I had put the children to bed, I came out into the hall as Jean was passing. We caught each other by surprise and when our eyes met there was a surge of desire flowing in our glance. Magnetism flung us together in a passionate embrace of kissing and caressing as if we had been starving for it. Tears streamed down my face as I trembled with the knowledge that he would surely refuse me, while my heart cried out to cling to him forever.

He drew back, his eyes shining with joy, and then a frown clouded his brow.

"Why the tears," he asked tenderly.

I only sobbed more and couldn't answer for several minutes. Finally I looked at him and spoke. "Please, I know you would not touch me like this if you knew everything about me."

"But why? I have loved you for all these long months, waiting only to touch you like this. Why would you deny me now? Was I wrong to think you wanted it as well?"

"No," I shook my head violently. "I did want it. I will always want it, but..."

"For God's sake, woman! Do you mean to drive me mad? What could possibly stand between us? If you love me as I love you, then we should be married and care for each other always."

"It is not so simple as that. I can never marry you." I wanted to add, as long as Lord Blackney is alive, but I held my tongue.

"Then you do not love me?" He was crestfallen. His eyes met mine in such an agony of sorrow that I began to weep again and threw myself into his arms.

"If only you could know how much I love you, how much I long to be your wife and live with you always," I sobbed, "but there are things I have not told you. Things I have not dared to tell you for fear the Inquisition would torture you into revealing them one day. They would destroy me. Please try to understand." I stood miserably before him.

"I believe you do love me," he touched my hair gently and brushed it out of my eyes. "I can see that you are suffering as much as I am." Now tears filled his eyes as well and he held me close in his arms. "Are you married already then, Isobel?" He asked the question stiffly.

I could only nod as I pushed away from him.

"Aye, there is too much pain in this life for all of us. We shall fare better in the next, God willing." He shook his head sadly, crossing himself. "You know I cannot let you stay here like this now. It would not be right. I will find another place for you. I have friends who can help." With a defeated smile, he touched my tear-streaked cheek. "Will you promise to meet me again in heaven, sweet Isobel? If I can look forward to that, my pain will be endurable."

"Heaven!" I turned on him with a sneer, almost spitting the word. "Why do we have to wait for some imaginary heaven when we could have heaven right now?" I ran to the window and looked out at the darkening sky, a sense of foreboding clenching at my gut. "I will never be safe once I leave you."

Jean reached out and pulled me violently to his breast, moaning with anguish. "I will be only a shell of a man without you, Isobel, but we cannot stay together like this. If you are another man's wife I dare not keep you near. My passions might cause me to act in ways we would both regret." He kissed me again, long and hot, then flushed and turned away. "Even now I cannot control the love you arouse in me." He frowned in confusion. "I cannot see how it could be wrong."

"Then why do you believe it is?" I glared at him defiantly. "Can you not trust your own heart? Or do you care more for your honor among men than you care for me?"

Jean hesitated. "I care only for our immortal souls, Isobel." He stood gazing sadly at me, helpless and frustrated.

Suddenly I felt as though miles stretched between us. "I will leave then." I spoke abruptly. "Tell the children goodbye for me, and that I will always love them." I hurried off to pack my belongings.

"Where will you go?" Jean followed after me, torn between anguish and longing.

"What do you care?" I shrugged, "I suppose I will travel again as I did before I came here with Solomon. I will survive."

"Isobel," his voice was a whisper. "Will you not let me find a place for you where it is safe? If you tell fortunes you are throwing your life away. The spies of the Inquisition are everywhere now."

"There is no safe place for me, Jean. I have only just realized that now. It does not matter where I go."

Jean bowed his head. "I am only doing what I feel is best for both of us, for our eternal salvation. Please know that I will always love you, Isobel."

I sighed deeply. "Isobel is my daughter's name. I cannot tell you my own." My heart felt like it was breaking. "I will always remember your kindness."

He pressed a purse of gold into my hand and then, with tears in his eyes, he embraced me until I gathered the strength of will to push him away. I ran out into the night with shuddering sobs. Sloe was alert and waiting when I entered her pasture.

Ralph closed the diary there, feeling thoroughly exhausted. It was a relief to him that Carmen had left her new love. It wouldn't have been right for her to find comfort in this life of sin she had chosen when she abandoned her husband. But something about the way Julia had described the scene of their parting made him feel agitated. Such depth of passion was beyond anything he had ever experienced. It made him wonder. Julia certainly seemed to know a lot for an eighteen-year-old kid. Maybe there really was some truth to this reincarnation stuff.

CHAPTER 24

Space

Nostalgia hung thick around Julia as she rinsed her feet in the icy stream beside her hut. Each moment of this last morning must be savored. Now it was time to reenter the life she had run away from, but not without paying a final homage to the wilderness. She would never be able to return in quite the same way. That much she knew.

Grandma had offered her a place to stay and had even found her a few house cleaning jobs. That would make the transition a little easier. Cleaning houses was not Julia's idea of fun, but it was a quick way to earn a living and she could save money for a place of her own. Besides, it was a good way to meet new people. That might be less awkward than trying to reconnect with inquisitive friends from her old neighborhood.

She stretched her arms and legs and got to her feet, taking one last look around. It was harder to leave than she had expected. It felt as if she was saying goodbye to Margaret Littlewolf all over again — and that goodbye held an echo of the pain of leaving Melita and her daughter so long ago.

Frank was puttering about inside the hut, trying to make himself useful. "I think I've got everything ready to go," he announced enthusiastically as he stepped out the door. "I'm just waiting for you."

"Yeah, I guess it's time. It may take all day to catch a ride, so we'd better go." She forced a smile.

They shouldered their heavy backpacks and began trudging up the hill toward the road. The bubbling of the stream faded away as the crunching of leaves and gravel underfoot became a rhythmic pulse. Julia glanced at Frank as he walked beside her. His face was solemn.

"What are you thinking about?" Her voice almost startled him.

Frank glanced up abruptly and shrugged. "The future, I guess. I don't really know what I'll do once I get back to town. To tell you the truth, I've been happier here than I've ever been in my entire life."

"Why don't you stay then? I'm not expecting you to go with me."

"It wouldn't be the same without you. It's probably you that made it so wonderful."

Julia was silent for a moment. The sound of their footsteps seemed to crash through the stillness.

"We'll still be friends, Frank. You'll know where to find me."

"But it won't be the same. I won't have you all to myself like I did here. If it were up to me, we'd just stay here forever. Who needs the rest of the world?"

"Geez, Frank! We've been through this again and again. It would be totally impractical over the winter."

"Yeah, I know, but it sure would be fun to try it."

"You're not going to give up, are you? You're afraid to even touch me, but you think we should live together for the rest of our lives. I don't get it." She watched his jaw tighten. "You know I care for you, Frank, but — I don't know. Let's not complicate things."

"It's Tom, isn't it? In your mind he's perfect. I'm just flesh and blood, human, but that's not good enough for you. I'm not spiritual enough. You need some sort of ghost to get you off."

"Frank!" The intensity in Julia's voice shook him. "Leave Tom out of this. It has nothing to do with him."

"Well," he spoke more cautiously, "it sure changed your attitude that day when you were all ready to crawl into my pants. Your little séance session put a real damper on your ardor."

"Maybe it just woke me up, Frank. Maybe it made me realize that what I felt for you was just animal magnetism. Maybe it reminded me of a different kind of connection that's far more satisfying than anything I could ever experience with you."

"Ouch! Okay, Okay," Frank held up his hands to ward her off. "You asked what I was thinking about, so I told you. Give me a break!"

"Sorry," she softened a bit. "I guess I — I got scared. I really messed things up with Tom. I thought I knew what I was doing, but now he's dead. So, I don't trust my own instincts anymore." She glanced at Frank to see if he was really listening. "It's going to take me some time to sort it all out. I just need a little space."

CHAPTER 25

Daniel Murphy

When Julia's grandmother met Frank Davis she was puzzled. He had arrived at her house with Julia, the two of them lugging backpacks, grimy and bedraggled after hitchhiking all day. Frank seemed nice enough, but there was something coarse about him. The way he spoke had a rough edge to it that irritated Carol. She aimed to surround herself with the finer things in life and Frank did not fit her idea of culture and refinement.

Julia seemed to be quite comfortable with the guy, though. Carol wondered what sort of relationship they shared. He certainly wasn't handsome. His thin sandy hair was longish and his chin was covered with reddish stubble. Fine lines had begun to etch themselves around his eyes, so he had to be at least ten years older than Julia. Maybe he was some kind of father figure. At any rate, he seemed harmless. A shower and shave might even make him look presentable.

Now that she finally had Julia safe at home, Carol wanted to relax and enjoy it. She wasn't going to let a little thing like Frank's presence spoil her mood. She even invited him to join them for dinner, which Frank accepted gratefully. He had a friend in town who had offered him a couch to sleep on, but that didn't include meals. A home-cooked dinner was more than he had bargained for.

Carol had already invited two other guests for dinner. She hadn't expected Julia to be back so soon, but saw no reason why they couldn't

117

all enjoy a meal together. Father Rosini, the pastor of her local Catholic church, and his new assistant pastor were expected at six o'clock. The assistant had just arrived from Ireland the day before. Carol didn't even know his name yet. As the priest's official housekeeper, Carol thought she should be the first one in the parish to welcome him into her home.

Julia and Frank were exhausted. After showering and putting on clean clothes they sat around the kitchen looking like lost kids. Carol put them to work chopping vegetables for salad and setting the table while she attended to the main dishes. All the while she was observing Frank with the curiosity of a biologist who had just come upon an unfamiliar species. She had to admit, Frank appeared to be very respectful of Julia. The two of them seemed to have a pleasant rapport.

Julia mechanically placed silverware around the table, letting her mind drift. She was very aware of her grandmother's curiosity about Frank. It was amusing. Frank was so unlike anyone Carol would have chosen to spend time with. He had no pretensions and cared little about appearances. In spite of that, or perhaps because of it, Julia could see that Carol found him fascinating.

She looked at the five place settings she had just laid out, trying to decide where she would like to sit. What bizarre twist of fate had brought her home on the very evening that Carol had two priests coming for dinner? One of them was a total stranger and the other an uneasy specter from her childhood. She remembered Father Rosini looming over her at communion as he placed the host in her hands. He was so tall.

Actually, Julia hadn't seen Father Rosini since the last time she had gone to Mass with her grandmother when she was about twelve years old. He had seemed like a giant then, but she figured he must have shrunk a little by now. He had to be nearly eighty. And of course she had grown taller. He would probably just seem like an ordinary guy. She could deal with that. The other one made her nervous. He might be intimidating. Some dedicated young priest with a thick Irish brogue she could barely understand — that could be awkward. They were always so zealous, those young ones. She just hoped they wouldn't have to talk about religion.

Julia decided that the place to the right of the foot of the table would be hers, with Grandma on her left and her back to the wall. That would feel safe. No strange priests would be hovering behind her. Just as she had made up her mind, the doorbell rang. She glanced at Frank as Carol pulled off her apron and rushed to the door. With any luck the guy from Ireland would be tired from his trip and their guests would leave early.

Father Rosini entered first, ducking his head slightly as he passed through the doorway. Damn! He was tall. His hair was still dark, though he had a distinguished sprinkling of gray about the temples. He didn't look a day over sixty. The other one stepped in after him with a shy glance around the room. His eyes caught for an instant as he met Julia's gaze, then moved on.

"My new assistant, Father Daniel Murphy," Father Rosini's deep voice resonated through the room as he pressed Carol's hand in his. "Carol McCullen."

"It's a pleasure to meet you," Carol greeted the young man with a warmth she reserved only for priests. She shook his hand and turned to introduce him to Julia and Frank.

Julia was still standing beside the table, a rush of blood flushing her cheeks. She found it hard to breathe. The air seemed to crush in on her and she could swear she smelled the fragrance of honeysuckle. Reality was wavering.

"My granddaughter, Julia," Carol's voice snapped Julia back to the present.

"Oh, hello. I'm glad you could join us." Julia muttered the correct words, but her mind was racing to pinpoint the source of her disquiet. Images from the distant past were swimming through her head, but she couldn't make sense of them.

It would only be a few minutes before these awkward formalities were finished. Then she could drift to the sidelines and watch. As those minutes ticked by, she found herself feeling more and more uncomfortable. At last she heard her grandmother announce that dinner was ready. Finally, something to do. Something she didn't have to think about.

With relief, Julia headed toward the place she had so thoughtfully chosen at the table. Carol went to the chair at the head of the table and offered it to Father Rosini. Frank came to Julia's rescue and took the seat on her right before the other priest could claim it, not that he seemed to have any intention of doing so. He was engaged in a lively conversation with Carol as he settled into the seat directly opposite Julia.

"I've been lookin' farward to this all day," he spoke perfectly good English, with a light, lilting brogue. Sincerity exuded from his face.

It had to be an act, Julia figured. Why would he be looking forward to having dinner with three complete strangers and one person he had only met the day before? He was nice enough looking, with fine features and a ruddy glow to his cheeks. His dark hair was thick, almost shaggy, and his aquamarine eyes sparkled when he smiled.

There was something so familiar about him. Not the way he looked, but something in his glance that echoed far back in time. Julia watched him closely. This was someone she had known before, someone she had known well, but where and when? And why in hell was he a priest?

CHAPTER 26

Housekeeping

Three weeks after Julia settled in at her grandmother's house, Carol tripped and broke her hip. It would take several weeks to heal, so she asked her granddaughter to take over her housekeeping and cooking duties at the priest's house until she recovered. It was with some trepidation that Julia agreed, though she did have a mild curiosity about what went on in the private lives of priests.

Both priests were away when she first arrived at their house, so she took a quick look around. It was a Victorian style house, with dark wood paneling in most of the rooms. The living room had a view of the busy downtown shopping area. Julia watched pedestrians passing by as she ran the vacuum cleaner over the carpet. It was the sort of carpet old ladies had in their parlors, with soft pastel leaf designs and burgundy flower patterns around the border. The chairs and sofa were thickly upholstered in plush wine-colored velvet, and a heavy walnut coffee table occupied the center of the room, covered with papers and magazines. It was all rather impersonal, as if the real lives of the residents took place somewhere else.

She supposed Father Rosini had no interest in decor. It looked as though nothing had changed in fifty years. Obviously he didn't let Carol exercise her decorating abilities here. Still, it was a clean, cozy home with a pleasant ambiance.

It wasn't long before Father Rosini walked in. He settled himself in an office off the living room and leafed through religious journals while Julia prepared lunch.

"Father Murphy will be in later, so put something aside for him, will you?" Father Rosini's voice boomed out. "I'll take my lunch in here if you don't mind."

"No problem," she called back, glad that the kitchen was on the opposite side of the living room from his office.

As long as he kept his distance, things would be fine. He wasn't the sort of person she wanted to get close to. Damn, he was tall! And he always seemed so serious. She couldn't remember ever hearing him laugh, but maybe he just didn't have anything to laugh about.

She arranged his sandwich, soup, and salad on a tray and poured him a glass of red wine. Grandma said he always had to have wine with his lunch and dinner. Not such a bad life, Julia thought. Someone else does the cleaning and cooking. All the priests have to do is say Mass and talk to people all day. It could be a lot worse. But then, they had to take vows of celibacy and obedience. That didn't sound so good.

Julia observed Father Rosini carefully as she placed the lunch tray on his desk. He barely grunted an acknowledgment and continued to read his magazine. As she studied his face she concluded that sex was probably the furthest thing from his mind. Besides, who would ever be attracted to him anyway?

She put away the lunch supplies and began to dust the dining room. Grandma had told her it was important to check the bedrooms to make the beds and pick up dirty laundry, but she was putting it off. Couldn't these guys do anything for themselves? It was obvious that Carol believed in spoiling them rotten. According to Grandma, they had more important things on their minds than picking up after themselves. Yeah, right!

Julia's thoughts were interrupted by the sound of the front door opening. In walked Father Murphy with a bemused smile on his face. A sudden look of surprise flashed in his eyes as he noticed Julia.

"Well, good afternoon to ya. Julia, isn't it?"

"Yeah. Hi," she shrugged awkwardly. "My grandmother broke her hip, so I'm filling in for her."

"Oh no! I'm sorry ta hear that. Will she be all right?" He looked genuinely concerned.

"They say she'll be back on her feet in a couple of months. It was a pretty clean break I guess."

"Well, it's nice of ya ta take over for her. Looks like you're doin' a splendid job." His smile returned. "Is there anything ta eat? I'm starved."

"I'll have to heat up your soup, but everything else is ready." Julia headed for the kitchen.

"Oh, don't bother. I'm not an invalid." He gave her a wink as he turned to open the refrigerator. "Your grandmother probably told ya ta wait on us hand and foot, but as long as I'm an able-bodied man I'll do a few things fer meself now and then."

Julia grinned. He was charming. Such a relief after the somber presence of Father Rosini. She viewed him from the back as he poured his soup into a saucepan. He certainly was an able bodied man, she thought to herself. He was wearing an ordinary pullover sweater with black slacks, rather than the Roman collared shirt he had worn to her grandmother's house. He looked like a regular guy.

"How do you like America by now?" Julia asked after a pause.

He turned with a curious gaze, his eyes catching hers for an instant before he looked back at the soup. "I'm gettin' used to it. Thank ya for askin'." He gave a little laugh. "Everything is so much faster here."

"I've heard that Ireland is really beautiful. You must miss it."

"Oh, I do, but I'm so busy I don't have time ta be homesick. Besides, there's so much ta explore and discover here. It's excitin'."

He looked her way again and she blushed when their eyes met.

"Well, I'd better get back to work," she excused herself abruptly.

She grabbed the vacuum cleaner and started down the hall. What was it about this guy that seemed so familiar? It was the same feeling she had when she first met him. They had been friends once, good friends. That much she knew. But where and when? And why couldn't she remember?

CHAPTER 27

Escape

Every time Ralph intended to continue reading Julia's diary, something would get in the way. It was usually his scruples. He had been feeling so guilty about invading Julia's privacy that he even asked a priest about it in his confession. The priest seemed to think there was nothing wrong with reading the diary of a missing girl if it might help to locate her. Ralph was not totally convinced, but he felt a bit less guilty as he picked up the little volume again and began to read.

> *I paid no attention to where I rode that night. Sloe took me where she pleased. I felt as though my heart was broken. I could not even think fondly of Jean for comfort. He had only wanted a wife, not a friend. My love and my pain counted for nothing. I didn't fit within the rules of his religion, so he cast me off like so much baggage. Sure, he was doing the right thing by all external standards, but what about love? What about his inner truth? How happy could his heaven be if he threw away what he really wanted, the thing his soul was longing for?*
>
> *With reckless abandon, I rode through the towns, telling fortunes in the public squares. If the Inquisition was after me, let them take me. Damn them! I would not run and hide anymore.*

It wasn't long before those Dominican devils heard the rumors. The witch with the black mare was again telling fortunes, undermining the faith of their followers. Damn them again! Ten men they sent to take me! Ten men with swords in hand, as if I was a dangerous criminal. Like a prize they carried me off to a church where they imprisoned women and children. All night I could hear the screams of those they tortured in rooms I could not see. Horrible screams. I wondered when my turn would come, but a worse torture was in store for me.

Two days after I was captured I heard a voice outside the door that made my blood freeze. Hugh Blackney had come to take his wife home.

"There cannot be a God who would allow this," I told myself. "Let me die. Torture me, but not this."

His face was lined and hard when he came in, those lifeless, gray eyes set like stone. My impulse was to run, but I was trapped. I stood staring at him as if all the demons of hell were after me.

"Carmen," he smiled ever so slightly, "it is time for you to come home with your husband. Or," he lowered his voice to a whisper, "would you rather burn?"

"I will take my chances here," I answered without meeting his gaze."

"Ha," he turned to his audience of guards. "She thinks she has a choice." Then looking back at me he growled, "Whether you choose it or not, you will be my wife, AND," he was shouting now, "you will bear my sons!"

He gestured to his men and they tied me with ropes and dragged me out to Blackney's wagon where I was loaded on like a piece of luggage. On the long ride home I tried to remember all the spells Melita had taught me. She had told me about one that would make a man impotent, but

I couldn't remember it. Somehow I had to get in touch with her.

We stopped for a night at an inn. I was carried into a room with bars on the windows and a bolted door, but I could see people walking by outside. In vain I tried to get someone to rescue me, but no one even turned to look when I called out. It wasn't long before Lord Blackney had finished his meal and he came to share my room and my bed.

"You will not escape me so easily this time, dear wife," his voice sent shivers through my bones. He pulled me roughly to him and tore off my clothes, pushing me down on the bed.

I had no reservations about screaming now. I screeched long and loud until I thought his ears would burst. My reward was a fat hand clapped over my mouth and nose, so I couldn't breathe. I must have turned blue by the time he let go. It felt as if my eyes would pop out of my head. I hated him.

I was half faint and dizzy from lack of air as he climbed on top of me. Every cell in my body cried out for Melita. Why couldn't I remember the spell she had taught me? I clamped my eyes shut, tears streaming into my ears.

Suddenly the world took a spin. I smelled a hint of honeysuckle in the air. The body on top of me felt lighter. Firm supple muscles seemed to ripple against my skin. The hairy prickles became gentle caresses. Warm lips melted into my neck and cheek and mouth. I drank the nectar of love, feeling orgasms bursting in my heart and throat and out the top of my head.

"Leo!" I whispered his name aloud. I did not bother to wonder how he had got there. It was enough to know his spirit was with me, somehow. Delicious, infinitely tender kisses warmed the coldness in my gut, healing all the pain of

*a lifetime. I fell asleep as blissful as an angel. Maybe there
was a God after all.*

*When I awoke there was no sign of Hugh Blackney. My
clothes were torn and tossed about, but it seemed as though
my husband had simply walked out without harming me.
It was a miracle. I knew Melita had come through for me
after all.*

*That morning Lord Blackney sent his men in to tie me
up and load me onto his wagon. He did not say a word to
me, but I saw him look my way with a frown. I wondered
what he was thinking. We traveled all day in silence, and
I began to remember the spell I needed. By the time we
arrived at Blackney's estate that evening it was clear in my
mind.*

*I had to send servants to collect the ingredients, since I
was confined to the house with guards at every exit, but it
wasn't long before I had what I needed. I felt the support of
Melita and Leo with me as I whispered the binding chant,
spinning energy in a spiral above my head. I ground herbs
and hair against wood and stone, feeling their essence flow
through me. When I was done I wrapped it all in a piece of
cloth from the hem of my dress to make an amulet. I knew
I was now protected from Hugh Blackney. His power over
me would be withered. I could hardly wait until he came
for me and felt the power of my spell.*

*I kept my amulet with me at all times, tucked in a
tiny pocket in my skirt. If he so much as touched me his
virility would wither, but the amulet did nothing to appease
his anger. He soon realized that something was amiss and
suspected that I was responsible for his impotent state. Yet
there was nothing he could prove. He had me watched even
more closely. At night he locked me in my room with a
guard outside my door. Even so I managed to escape.*

One night when the moon was dark I heard a whisper at my window calling my name. The sound of that voice filled me with rapture.

"Leo!" I wanted to shout it, but it came out quiet as a breeze. Rushing to the window, I reached through and pulled his face to mine, kissing him long and full on the mouth. He grinned.

"I am happy to see you, too, Carmen," his eyes flashed with joy, "but I need to get you out of here before I make love with you."

Suddenly I was worried. "If Lord Blackney catches you he will kill you, Leo. Do not risk your life for me."

"Without you, Carmen, I have no use for life." His dark eyes met mine with startling frankness. "Come now. I brought a rope ladder for you to climb down."

I looked out the window at the sheer three storey drop below and then back at Leo. "All right, I trust you. What do I have to lose?"

The ladder was made of flimsy rope. I didn't even want to know how he had got it up to my window. Together we made our way to the ground and out through the main gate. We left so quietly that the dogs did not even notice our passing. Leo took my hand and led me quickly into the woods. There, to my great surprise and delight, was Sloe, my black mare. I threw my arms around her neck as she nickered and rubbed her forehead against me. With tears streaming down my face I turned to Leo.

"How did you find her? I thought I would never see her again."

Romanies know their horses. I heard rumors and followed her trail. That was easy. Finding you was not so easy." He looked up at the sky, noting the position of the stars. "We have no time to waste. Let us be off."

We rode fast and far that night and the following day, until we reached a camp where familiar faces greeted us. I felt safer there than I had felt in years. Leo and I sat by the campfire, exhausted, while Melita spread food before us. My little Isobel had grown to be a beautiful girl. She greeted me shyly, with curiosity. I longed to hold her in my arms, but to her I was a stranger.

A young boy crawled into Leo's lap and I noticed how much alike they were. I looked abruptly at Leo with a chill in my bones.

"Where is your wife?"

He met my gaze sadly. "She was taken by the Inquisition and burned as a witch." He pressed his lips tightly together, fighting back tears. "There was nothing I could do."

Rage boiled in my blood. That beautiful innocent young woman could never have deserved such a fate. There was a terrible feeling of helpless anger in all the hearts gathered around that fire. We were no match for the power of the church.

Someone began singing and clapping a slow rhythm and one voice after another joined in. A sad song seemed to swell out of the mood of sorrow. These people could even make tragedy beautiful. Another song followed, then another livelier one. Soon we were all clapping and dancing as we sang. The mood became happy and laughter filled the night.

Leo took his little son to his vardo, but returned a short while later, stamping his feet and clapping hands above his head as he danced up to me. I couldn't help but notice how handsome he was, a mature man now in the prime of his life, no longer the young lad I had once loved. He circled round me gazing into my eyes, beating time to the music with his feet. An old woman wailed a song from the depths of her soul.

It was a love song they were singing, but I didn't understand all the words. I only knew it was meant for me and this beautiful man who danced with me. I smiled, moving in time with him, echoing the arc of his arm and the stamping of his feet. It seemed as if our bodies flowed together in one movement. The faces around us were grinning. They could feel it, too.

That night I slept in Leo's arms like a baby. I had never felt so happy in all my life.

CHAPTER 28

Heaven

L ate autumn sent crisp breezes cutting through the warm afternoons, silencing the crickets and mosquitoes that had enlivened the Indian summer nights. Julia's nineteenth birthday had come and gone. To her it seemed like an eternity since she had turned eighteen.

Carol's hip was mending well, but she had developed a case of pneumonia and had to stay in the hospital for longer than anticipated. Her doctor had ordered her to take another month off from work to regain her strength. Julia was glad to handle Carol's occasional decorating jobs, with her grandmother's advice, and she carried on with the housekeeping duties at the priest's house.

The presence of Father Murphy continued to unsettle her. More often than not, he seemed to avoid her, though he was always cheerful and friendly when they met. He rarely would let his eyes meet hers, but there was one time when she caught him by surprise. He had come home earlier than usual that day and gone straight to his room in a rush. Julia was there washing the windows. She turned with a gasp when he flung the door open, just in time to see sparks leap into his eyes. Blushing deeply, he turned and headed for the bathroom.

That moment had shaken Julia. She had seen that look before and she knew what it meant. Father Murphy wasn't just a priest after all. He was a man with a heart. He could feel longing and love. It wasn't just Julia's imagination that kept her awake at night. He was feeling it, too.

Quickly, she gathered up her cleaning supplies and left the room. It was always awkward being in there, but now it felt absolutely oppressive. She had to get outside. There was a small garden behind the house where Father Rosini grew flowers in the summer. Now they were all turning brown, except for the mums and asters, which bloomed in great profusion. Julia sucked in cool air, feeling it soothe her burning cheeks. A faint smell of honeysuckle seemed to drift on the breeze, but the honeysuckle had long since lost its blooms. For an instant Julia felt herself dancing in the light of a campfire, somewhere long ago. Then it passed.

She sat on the little garden bench where the sun shone in dappled patches through the trees. Her flaming hair rose on the breeze. With eyes closed, she leaned back against the fence, feeling quite alone. From an upstairs window Daniel Murphy watched her with a lump in his throat, but she would never know. He spent the rest of the afternoon in his room.

Daniel Murphy was watching again the next day when Frank came to pick Julia up after work. He saw how they hugged outside the house and walked to Frank's car arm in arm. It was hard to believe she could be in love with Frank, but in a way Daniel hoped she was. That would make it so much easier for him.

Frank hadn't seen Julia in weeks. He'd been out of town on a construction job. Now that he was making money, Frank had rented a little house on the outskirts of town. He didn't see why Julia couldn't move in with him just to see how things would work out. He planned to bring up the idea after he took her out to dinner. They had so much in common, even though he was a lot older. It felt to him like they were meant for each other.

He had chosen a nice restaurant, with crisp mauve tablecloths, three forks and crystal wine glasses at each place setting. Frank was impressed with himself. It had been a long time since he had dined in such elegance. In fact, he wasn't sure he had ever had so many people waiting on him at once. He watched Julia, wondering if she was enjoying herself. She seemed preoccupied, like something was bothering her, but Frank decided not to pry. She would tell him when she was good and ready. That much he had learned about her.

When he invited her to see his new place after dinner she seemed almost excited. That was promising. He was so encouraged that, when they arrived, he picked her up and carried her over the threshold, but that made her indignant.

"What the hell are you doing, Frank?" She struggled to get her feet on the floor. "I'm not your damn wife."

"I thought it would be funny." He shrugged it off. This was not getting off to a good start.

"Geez! You have a strange sense of humor," she pretended to snarl at him, shaking her head. Her quick laugh eased the tension. "So show me the house already."

She marched off toward the kitchen, snooping into every corner on the way. It was a decent house, comfortable in a classic Craftsman style, with a large front porch and gabled windows in the attic. Julia liked it.

"Hey, it's great," she said, turning to smile at Frank. "Congratulations!"

Frank gazed at her with awkward anticipation. "You could live here too, if you wanted," he spoke hesitantly. "There's plenty of room."

"Wait a minute. Let's just back up and pretend you didn't say that." She looked at him directly.

Reality was shifting. Layers of memories danced before her eyes. She felt so odd standing there, as if she had been in that exact spot before, and yet it was another time, another place. A great longing welled up inside of her and then a sharp pain in her heart. Searing pain. She had to leave. It felt like this man was sending her away, rejecting her, though he claimed to love her.

"Oh my god," she gasped. "I have to get out of here. This is too weird."

She turned toward the door almost tripping over Frank's feet in her hurry, but his hands reached out to stop her.

"Wait, Julia. You're scaring me." He pulled her close and wrapped his arms around her. "Tell me what's going on."

Julia looked into Frank's eyes once and then closed her eyes. The world was spinning. His lips brushed against hers and she opened her mouth to drink him in. She knew that kiss. It stabbed her heart painfully.

"Stop it," she gasped, pushing him away. Anger flooded through her. Now she remembered everything. "You had your chance with me and you threw it away. I would have given anything to live with you, but all you cared about was your honor and your stupid religion. Where is your honor now, Frank?"

"What are you talking about? What religion? I'm not religious." Frank looked at her as if she had gone mad, but something inside of him almost remembered.

"You told me you would wait for us to meet again in heaven." Her breath came fast. "Well, this is it. Is this what you wanted, Frank? Is this the heaven that you sacrificed your dreams for? Is it?"

"Julia, you're not making sense. I don't know how to answer." Frank was dazed. She sounded crazy, but somehow he felt she was right. He let his hands slip from around her waist as she backed away from him.

"Welcome to heaven, Jean Ferrier." Julia turned and ran out into the night. Her heart was bursting in anguish.

For a long time Frank sat on the corduroy-covered sofa in his new living room thinking about what Julia had said. Jean Ferrier was not a name that meant anything to him. Perhaps it was some character in a novel or a historical figure, but what did it have to do with him? And what was all this about heaven? He didn't even believe in heaven.

Still, she was right in a way. It seemed like he had always been waiting for her, as if hoping for some heavenly reunion. Now he realized there would never be a fairytale ending. No happily ever after. But Julia must care at least. Otherwise she wouldn't have been so angry.

CHAPTER 29

Vows

Julia seemed sullen the next morning when she arrived at the priest's house. Father Murphy was heading out the door as she came in. She greeted him with a cool detachment, for which he was glad. It was not a morning on which he wanted to play the role of charming employer.

The night had been torturous. The young priest had tossed and turned, praying for sleep. When it finally came he had dreamed of Julia. He hadn't been able to get her out of his mind. Now he walked the city streets pondering his dilemma. If he stuck around, matters would surely get worse, unless he fired her, but that would take some explaining. She was doing an excellent job as housekeeper and he really couldn't find any fault with her otherwise.

He could talk to her, tell her what was bothering him and ask her to leave voluntarily, but that might backfire. It would mean being alone with her and revealing his most intimate feelings. He wasn't sure he could handle that. Just the thought of it made his heart quiver. And what if she told him that she felt the same way he did? He sighed to himself. His one hope was that Carol would recover quickly, before his feelings escalated beyond control.

He tried convincing himself that he didn't love Julia — couldn't love her. He forced her out of his mind a thousand times a day, but now she moved into his subconscious, always watching, always waiting. She appeared in his dreams, gazing at him with shining eyes, and he gazed back. He couldn't stop what was happening in his dreams. And then he would find himself wide-awake, feeling as though she was melting into him, like they had been lovers for a thousand years.

Daniel had taken vows and now he questioned them. What did they really mean? He hadn't vowed not to love. Certainly, he could never marry, but there were so many other possibilities. His vows included abstaining from sex, but what about other ways of making love? He was experiencing those other ways as surely as if Julia was there in his arms. She seemed to sweep over him like a tide, merging with his soul in rapturous communion. How could sex be any more intimate than that?

And what was the point of his vows anyway? Were they meant as a sacrifice to atone for his sins, or were they merely a way to make sure priests would not be preoccupied with the duties of family life? Or, he pondered all possible motives, was it sheer aversion by the church founders — aversion to the physical world, aversion to women and to the body with all its desires and functions?

He had read something by an Indian guru saying that the church promoted a negative attitude toward sex in order to control people. The article implied that if people knew the hidden power of their sexual energy they would find their own path to God. They would no longer be dependent on the church and its priests for their spiritual guidance. He had pushed that idea aside without really thinking about it. Now he began to wonder. It was all feeling too complicated.

Daniel began to question the very concept of God. Was God some cruel being that had created humans with romantic and sexual desires only to forbid them to follow them? Or had God made a mistake? What was God anyway? They say, "God is love." But what is love? There are too many definitions to count.

Maybe that is the key. God or love is too big and too varied to define. It is whatever we perceive in the moment. Maybe God IS this moment, this anguished, ecstatic, intense moment. Maybe that's all there really is — an endless moment of ever-shifting experience.

Could it be that the church was misleading millions of people, or was it truly the infallible institution he had been raised to believe it was? Could such an external authority even begin to define one's inner morality? And what about ecstasy? These moments of rapturous communion with Julia, even in her physical absence, were the closest Daniel had ever felt to knowing God. Wasn't God supposed to be alive in Julia and in himself? Didn't the love he felt come from God? God moving through him?

In the seminary everything had seemed so clear and easy to accept. He had wanted to be a priest most of his life. His parents had strongly steered him in that direction from early childhood. It had seemed like his destiny. But that was before he met Julia.

After three hours of walking and brooding, Daniel Murphy returned home. Julia was washing dishes in the kitchen. She seemed troubled and looked as though she hadn't slept in days. It was hard to walk past her without patting her reassuringly on the shoulder.

CHAPTER 30

Connection

There were only a few more pages of Julia's diary left to read when Ralph finally settled down to finish it. So far it had given him no real clue to her whereabouts, but it was the only hope he had left. He had gone back once again to that hut in the forest, but it had appeared to be abandoned. Now his only connection with her seemed to be in the pages of the little book he held in his hands.

Almost a year had gone by before Lord Blackney picked up my trail again. This time his anger knew no bounds. He hunted me down relentlessly, had me thrown in prison, and captured many of my Romani friends for good measure. Leo was dragged off to a dungeon where they tortured him to the point of death. I could hear his screams from my cell. At the end they came for me, those tonsured monks in their black-hooded cowls, carrying torches to light their way. They pushed me into a long dark hallway and led me down stone stairs to the tiny pit of filth where they had thrown Leo. He lay bleeding and broken in the slime of human excrement. Above him stood Hugh Blackney with a malicious leer on his face.

"Come to rescue your lover, have you?" He sneered in my face. "What can your magic do now, witch?"

I fell to my knees, leaning over the mangled body of the dearest friend I had ever known. It was my fault he had fallen into the hands of the Inquisitors. I pulled his head onto my lap and stroked his hair, whispering words of comfort in his Romani tongue. His eyes met mine in a flicker of recognition. Then they went blank. He was gone. I moaned as my soul rose with his to a place free from all pain and fear. Then, forcing a tight smile, I wiped the tears from my cheeks. No one could hurt him anymore.

Noticing my smile, Lord Blackney slapped me sharply across the face, shocking me into awareness of my surroundings. They couldn't hurt Leo anymore, but now I became their prime target. I glared at my husband, vowing with all my soul to destroy him even from beyond the grave. My curse would follow him as long as he had the audacity to exist!

I was abruptly dragged to a dimly lit hall for my sham of a trial. The monks had stripped me naked and shaved my entire body, their lecherous fingers probing my flesh as they performed their so-called sacred duty to the church. My only relief was knowing that Leo would not have to witness the horrors I endured. All my long, black hair lay strewn over the floor.

Lord Blackney took a seat to the side of the room while I was made to stand shivering in the center. The monk who seemed to be in charge accused me of every vile act that his evil mind could imagine. When I would not confess to his accusations he had me beaten and pinched with hot metal tongs until I bled. There was not a spot on my skin that was not burned or bloody. But they did not kill me. No, they were saving that for later. My death would be a public spectacle for all to witness.

I had smelled the stench of burning flesh many times as I passed through small towns where the Inquisitors had plied their trade. Most often the victims were women, many of them old and wealthy, whose husbands had died or gone off to war. Fueled by self-righteous piety, greed, and unbridled fear of what they could not understand or control, the Inquisitors pillaged the wealth of hapless widows. They burned out the wisdom of the peasant folk, replacing it with fear of the almighty Catholic church.

(In those bone-fires hundreds of thousands of people burned. We call them bonfires now, but originally they were burning bones — bones of animals, bones of people. I've been doing some reading about it. Eighty-five percent of the people they burned were women. I was only one of many, and I remember. How many of us have been reborn now who still remember? Did those devils think they could stamp out the truth so easily? Well guess what — we're back!)

It was cold when they led me out to the pyre. Hundreds of eyes peered at me from the crowd that had gathered to see me burn. Many of them were forced to watch. Some were hungry for the drama of agony and horror. What were they thinking? I could see fear in those faces, but also a gloating satisfaction that they had been spared my fate. They were the good ones, or so they thought.

Hugh Blackney walked by to take a ringside seat. The peasants moved like a wave to avoid him. I spat with a curse when he crossed in front of me and spattered his coat sleeve with my saliva. He wiped his arm without thinking, then looked at his hand where it was wet with my spit. He realized then that I had caught him in a spell. With a look of terror he rushed at me, but the executioner stepped between us blocking his way. It wouldn't do to have me killed before I could be properly executed.

After pushing Blackney back, the executioner turned and glanced at me to see if I was all right. It was a natural human impulse, but a big mistake for an executioner. His brown eyes flashed from behind the black mask. Now I wasn't just a job to him. I was a real person.

He had just saved my life and caught a glimpse of my humanity. But he still had to light the fire that would take my life away. I could see tears in his eyes as he touched his torch to the kindling beneath my feet. Flames leapt between us, but his heart cried out to me for forgiveness. Him I can forgive. (I forgive you even now. My sweet Tom, who would do anything to make up for the past, even though you don't remember why — I forgive you.)

Smoke choked me as heat seared my feet and legs. I screamed, but it seemed as if someone else was screaming. I was floating beside the executioner, trying to comfort him. Then I just drifted away. Leo was with me. Rapture was all I knew.

Now that I have come to the end of my story I am exhausted and enraged, but I'm also afraid. I recognize now who Hugh Blackney is in my present life. I see him every day and I have a ruthless desire to take revenge on him in the most brutal way possible.

Only last night I dreamed I was dumping his body into an open grave. Apparently I had murdered him in the dream, but I was disappointed that he hadn't suffered enough. Strange dream! When awake, I find myself thinking of ways to make him suffer as he made me suffer. Am I losing my mind?

He's not even the same person anymore, but when he looks at me I still want to scream and scratch his eyes out. I want to see him grovel in pain the way he made Leo grovel. I have to get out of here before I do something awful!

The diary ended abruptly there. Ralph was stunned. The only person she had been seeing every day was himself. That made his flesh crawl. The image of the butcher knife flashed in his mind, mysteriously lying on his bedroom floor. Had Julia actually come close to murdering him? He didn't want to think about it.

Even if he had been Hugh Blackney in a former life, which he doubted very much, he couldn't still be responsible for what he had done then. He didn't even remember it. But at least he now understood why Julia had disappeared so quickly. It gave him some relief to know that she had the sense to remove herself from the temptation to torture him.

Ralph mulled over the contents of Julia's diary for a long time, particularly the final paragraphs. He was now doubly anxious to track her down and confront her with his suspicions. He didn't want her popping up from behind when he least expected it.

CHAPTER 31

Discovery

C arol's pneumonia was getting much better, but her doctor recommended that she spend another day in the hospital so he could keep an eye on her. She called Ralph to let him know. He sounded relieved that she was close to coming home and told her he would visit that evening. What he didn't tell her was that he would also visit her house on his way to the hospital.

She had promised not to tell Ralph about Julia's return and had kept her word. Carol had only seen him a few times in the hospital since Julia had moved into her house, so it hadn't been difficult to keep the secret. But Ralph had his suspicions. He knew Julia was unlikely to come back to his house, but it was very possible that she would go to her grandmother's when she got tired of running — or maybe she had been there all along.

Now that he knew Carol would be away from home for another day, Ralph seized the opportunity to do a little snooping. Not having a key, he crawled in through her laundry room window. The house looked much the same as it had when he was there last, nearly six months ago. The kitchen was tidy. His mother never liked to leave a mess, even for a few minutes. Everything had to look like a photo in a *House & Gardens* magazine. Ralph chuckled, remembering how she had nagged him about cleaning his room as a child.

As he headed toward the living room, Bosco rushed in through his little dog door and began barking and nipping at Ralph's heels every step of the way.

"Shut the hell up, you little piglet!" Ralph snarled at the pug, giving him a kick in the side. He had never liked dogs and was especially impatient with small yappy types. Bosco yelped and backed away, still barking. Ralph shooed him into the laundry room and slammed the door, hoping none of the neighbors had heard the commotion. One of them must be looking after the dog and might come running at the sound of his barking. He could still hear muffled growls as he entered the hallway and began peering into the bedrooms.

As soon as he opened the door to the guest room he felt a surge of satisfaction. Nobody was there, but clothes were hanging over a chair and tossed across the bed. Sweatshirts, blue jeans, shorts and T-shirts were not the sort of attire his mother would wear. They had to be Julia's clothes. His pulse began to race as he realized how close she must be. Was she stalking him or just trying to hide?

Impatient for answers, Ralph drove to the hospital and rushed to Carol's room.

"I know where Julia is hiding," he confronted her as soon as their greetings had been exchanged. "Why didn't you tell me?" He fixed her with an icy stare. "Has she been staying with you this whole time?"

"You were in my house?" She asked incredulously. "Did you break in? Well," she shrugged when he just glared at her, "I suppose you had to find out sooner or later. Julia asked me not to tell you and I respected her wishes. When she wants to see you I'm sure she will let you know."

"Oh no! This is too big for that. I'm not going to just wait around like a sitting duck until she decides my time is up."

"A sitting duck? What on earth are you talking about?" Carol began to cough and Ralph handed her a glass of water.

"I know this will sound strange, Mother," he continued, "but I think she tried to kill me. I need to find out where she is."

"Good lord, Ralph! Don't be so melodramatic. Why on earth would she want to kill you?"

"It's all in her diary," Ralph answered. "She has been plotting ways to torment me. She even killed me in a dream, but she thought I hadn't suffered enough. You can read it for yourself if you want to. She thinks I was her husband in some past life."

"Oh heavens! What were you doing reading her diary? I'm sure she was just making up stories."

"I read her diary, because it was the only clue I had that might help us find her." He paused with a flustered shake of his head. "Why do you think she just happened to disappear right after she left a knife on my bedroom floor? It's just too much of a coincidence."

"A knife? What kind of knife?" Carol was beginning to feel concerned.

"A butcher knife! She must have been intending to kill me, but changed her mind and ran away."

"You don't know that. There must be another explanation."

"The explanation is right there in her diary. She hated me and wanted me to suffer."

"And you're sure she was talking about you?"

"Who the hell else was she around every day? She lived in my house! And now she doesn't want you to tell me where she is. Doesn't that seem a little suspicious to you?"

"It does sound strange, but I'm not going to jump to conclusions. Maybe she was just trying to scare you."

"Well she did a damn good job of it," Ralph grumbled. Then, noticing his mother's agitation, he spoke more calmly. "See, you haven't read the diary. If she believed it was true, all that stuff she wrote in there, then she would have plenty of reason to want to kill me." He looked steadily at Carol with his jaw jutting forward. "I don't know if there's any truth to this reincarnation stuff she talks about, but she seems to believe it. She thinks I was responsible for having her burned as a witch and for having her lover tortured to death."

"Mother of mercy! Where does she get such ideas?" Carol clutched her throat, eyeing Ralph incredulously. "And you're thinking there may be some truth to all this?"

Ralph narrowed his eyes and looked at her straight on. "I really don't know, Ma, but it sure got me thinking."

"And to think you almost became a priest! Now you don't even believe in heaven anymore?" She threw up her hands in exasperation.

"Mother, the church doesn't deny the possibility of reincarnation. I asked a priest about it. He said it even seemed plausible to him."

"Well, I never heard of such a thing. But," she paused reflectively, "if that's what the priest said, what do I know?"

"Well, priests don't know everything, Ma," Ralph shook his head with an amused smirk. He had her going now.

"But even if this reincarnation thing is true," she stopped short with a frown, then gasped, "I don't think people are supposed to remember things like that. If we do live more than once, we should start off with a clean slate each time."

"But what if it doesn't always work that way? What if some people do remember? Julia can see things that other people can't see, like the way she knew when her parents were going to die. Maybe this is just another one of those things." Ralph leaned back in his chair expelling air through his nose forcefully. "If it was anyone but Julia I wouldn't give it a second thought, but she's different."

Carol looked at her son thoughtfully for several minutes. "All right, Ralph," she gave in. "Now that you know where she's living I suppose you'll find her sooner or later. Maybe now is as good a time as any. She's been taking over some of my duties while I've been laid up. Right now she's probably working at the Incarnation parish priest house, but don't go looking for her. I want to be there when you two meet."

The priest's house! That was the most unlikely thing Ralph had ever heard. It was the last place he would have thought to look for Julia. He left the hospital shaking his head in disbelief.

Now he would have to face her. There was no more putting it off, whether his mother liked it or not. Julia must still be angry with him or she would have called to let him know where she was. It might even be dangerous to meet her on his own, but he couldn't wait weeks for his mother to arrange a meeting. At least the priest's house was neutral territory, and hopefully the priests would be around to intervene in case she went ballistic. She wouldn't dare kill him in front of them.

When Ralph knocked at the front door of the priest's house his heart was pounding with apprehension. Father Rosini opened the door, car keys in his hand.

"Oh, hello Father. I'm sorry to disturb you, but I'm looking for my niece, Julia Flynn. I was told she was working here." Ralph spoke with forced calm. "It's kind of urgent."

"Come in. I'll let her know you're here on my way out the garage." Father Rosini turned abruptly and disappeared down a dark hallway.

A few moments later Julia appeared. Her brow was furrowed and her manner cautious, but she greeted her uncle cordially.

"Hello Uncle Ralph. I guess Grandma finally spilled the beans."

"No. I did some snooping around on my own." He said. "There is something I've been wanting to talk to you about."

"Oh, I bet there is," Julia sneered.

"It was me, wasn't it?" Ralph blurted the question out, quite to his own surprise. Then he looked at her anxiously.

Julia knew what he meant. "You've been doing some interesting reading lately?" She raised an eyebrow and waited for his answer.

"Yeah, I read it. I read your diary from cover to cover. You expected me to read it, didn't you?" He sounded defiant.

"Of course I did," she answered dryly. "But it's still an invasion of privacy."

"Hell, Julia! You threatened to kill me. Isn't that a lot worse than a little invasion of privacy?"

"That was just a dream, Ralph." Her voice was very quiet. "I wouldn't have actually murdered you."

"Then why was there a knife in my bedroom? Was that a dream too?"

Daniel Murphy was sitting in the kitchen eating a late lunch when Ralph arrived. He hadn't intended to eavesdrop, but there was something in the tone of Ralph's voice that made him wary. Who was this Ralph guy, anyway? And Julia sounded so tense. Something wasn't right.

He figured Julia would have a temper. Those Irish redheads often did. But murder? Had she really intended to kill the guy? She wasn't denying it. No matter. He must have done something to make her that angry. He trusted her that much, and he didn't trust Ralph one bit. Just the sound of Ralph's voice sent a chill up his spine.

The conversation seemed to be heating up as Father Murphy leaned closer to the door. He didn't want to make his presence known, but he felt that Julia might need his help.

"Why didn't you just come and talk to me, Julia?" Ralph's voice pleaded. "I'm not a horrible person. I've spent months going out of my mind wondering what happened to you, fearing the worst. And now I find out you've been at your grandmother's, like you've been there all along. How long have you been there, anyway?"

"That's none of your business, Ralph, and it's not the issue. I did try to talk to you. I tried for years before I remembered any of that stuff in my diary. You never listened. You were too caught up in yourself." Julia looked down at her hands with a sigh. "By the time I finished writing in the diary I was in no mood to talk. I just wanted to strangle you. I actually might have killed you if I had stayed any longer.

"The night I left, I woke up holding a knife to your throat. I was sleepwalking and I had no idea how I got there, or where I'd found the knife. I just dropped it and ran." She snorted a laugh to herself. "You should be glad I left when I did."

"All right," Ralph spoke slowly, as if to calm himself. "I am glad in a way, but... don't you think you should get some counseling or something? I mean, what if you get in this mood again? Should I be afraid for my life?"

"I would be if I was you." Julia looked him coolly in the eye.

Ralph felt a knot forming in his stomach. "Are you threatening me, Julia?"

"No. I'm just answering your question." She seemed extraordinarily calm and quiet, but her voice sounded constricted. "You destroyed me, Ralph. You had me burned at the stake. You tortured the man I loved until he died in agony. And I didn't get to forget it like you did. I had to relive it over and over and over again in this life until it almost drove me mad. Just because it happened in another lifetime doesn't mean you didn't do it, or that you can escape your karma."

"But even if that was true, which I doubt," Ralph spluttered, "it wasn't me. I don't remember any of it. I would never do those things. I'm not a monster."

"You don't want to remember, but that doesn't let you off the hook. You were definitely a monster in that lifetime and you will have to pay for it sooner or later."

Just then Daniel Murphy appeared in the doorway behind Julia. Ralph did a double take and blinked his eyes. For an instant he felt something familiar about the guy. Now he wasn't sure.

Julia turned, feeling a presence behind her. There was strength there to support her.

"Daniel?" She had never called him by his first name before. "Have you been listening to all this?"

"I overheard all I needed to. I'm here for ya, Julia. I don't know what this is all about, but I'll stand by ya." He reached out and took hold of her trembling hand.

"You have no idea how much that means to me," she whispered, choking back tears as she felt his warmth enveloping her.

Together the housekeeper and the priest stood confronting Ralph. There was no anger in their look, nor was there a threat, but Ralph felt like a damned man facing God. Suddenly he had a glimpse of the horrors of his past life and the pathetic unfolding of his present. Images of Carmen's face flashed before him, her head shaved and her body wreathed in flames. He backed slowly toward the door, feeling his way with outstretched arms. Once through, he turned and ran. As Julia watched, an ancient pain lifted from her heart. Hugh Blackney had no power to harm her anymore.

With deep gratitude she turned to face the man behind her. He moved with her as if in a dance, circling around her as he gazed into her eyes. Echoes of long ago flowed back and forth between them, like pulsing waves beating time to some forgotten music. It was unmistakable now. Julia was sure she smelled honeysuckle in the air.

Her focus sharpened as she gazed deeply into the eyes of Daniel Murphy. "I know who you are," she whispered. Her eyes were shining just like they always did in his dreams.

"Julia," Daniel gasped, stepping back abruptly, still gazing into her eyes. "Don't say any more."

He spun on his heel and rushed away down the hall. Overwhelming memories flooded through him. Hot, passionate images of young lovers in the woods made his heart ache and his blood race.

CHAPTER 32

Revelation

A sharp wind cut across Julia's face as she stood leaning against the railing of Frank's front porch. She let her eyes wander down the tree-lined street, feeling suddenly unsure. Frank was home. His radio blared country western music and she could hear him singing along. Julia smiled sardonically. She had come to ask Frank for help. Run to him almost, and now she only wanted to ridicule his music. It sounded so pitiful.

Maybe she was just looking for a reason not to knock on his door. After all, she was going to have to apologize for running out on him the last time she visited. That was a few days ago and she hadn't spoken to him since. Frank might be angry about that.

Julia had wanted to give Frank time to think about what she had said, hoping he would remember their past life together. Now she realized that he probably didn't have a clue. How could she expect him to remember what had happened in another lifetime? Most people didn't. But Frank had seemed to recognize her when they first met, even if only subconsciously. And now she needed him. There was nobody else she could turn to. She had to swallow her pride.

Frank wasn't all that thrilled to see Julia when she finally worked up the courage to knock on his door. He had expected an apology, or at least an explanation after she stormed out on him, but after hearing nothing from her for two days, he had let it go. At this point he was feeling wary of her, even wondering if she might be crazy.

Apologetically, Julia explained how she had suddenly recognized him as Jean Ferrier, her benefactor from a former lifetime.

"You were a wonderful man and I loved you," she told Frank," but you wouldn't let me stay with you, because of your religious beliefs — not after I told you I was married."

Frank began to soften. Her explanation seemed sincere enough, but he was still cautious. Seemed like every time he started getting close to Julia he got burned. He couldn't help but like her, though, and she seemed especially vulnerable today. Maybe it was even the perfect relationship for him. He would never have to worry about getting too close. That thought almost made him chuckle.

He felt a maddening attraction to this girl as she walked into his kitchen now, pulling her long red hair into a ponytail. Frank followed her, forgetting that he had been so annoyed. She glanced around the room with an approving eye. It was well organized and tidy.

Frank was in the midst of dinner preparation. Sliced onions and red bell peppers sizzled in a frying pan on the stove. The chopping board was covered with wedges of avocado, green chilis, mushrooms and a package of tortillas.

"Making fajitas? Looks good, Frank," she grinned.

Frank shrugged self-consciously, appreciating the compliment. It was rare that he felt genuine approval from anyone. "Thanks. You want a cup of tea? I just made a pot."

"You drink tea?" Julia teased. "I thought you'd be the beer type."

"It's a habit I picked up from my mother. She was English." He looked at her intently, suspecting she hadn't just come by for a cup of tea. "So what's up?"

"Nothing much," she shrugged. "It's just that things are getting kind of weird with my job. Well, my grandmother's job. I don't know if I want to go back. I mean it's not even my job, really. I'm only filling in until Grandma gets better, but — well, Ralph showed up today and told me that he had read my diary. I had written something about wanting to strangle him and that seemed to bother him." She smirked, glancing at Frank from the corner of her eye. "Should I go on?"

At first Frank's face registered surprise that Ralph would read her diary. Then his expression turned to shock. He was frowning incredulously.

"You really wanted to murder him?"

"I actually came pretty close one night, but that's a long story. I wasn't even awake."

"Yeah, I'd like to hear it sometime," Frank answered with one eyebrow raised.

Julia looked up to find him gazing at her curiously. For a long time they just stared at each other, hesitant smiles playing about their lips, until suddenly they both burst out laughing. They were beginning to feel a bit giddy now, a seductive camaraderie breaking through the tension.

"I don't know about this past-life stuff, Julia, but I definitely felt a jolt of something like recognition when I first met you — like I'd known you before and I'd been waiting to meet you again," Frank admitted. "I've never experienced anything like that with anyone else."

"Well, you did ask for it. You begged me to meet you in the next life." Julia answered. "You called it heaven, but this is about as close to heaven as we're going to get — for now anyway."

Frank pondered her words, renewing his speculations about life and death. Maybe he had lived before. Maybe Julia really did remember things they had shared long ago. It would sure make sense of their situation now — more sense than any other explanation he could come up with.

"So, we were in love with each other, but we didn't stay together because I was religious?" Frank snorted, frowning as he tried to imagine being in such a situation. "That sure wouldn't stop me now."

Julia laughed. "Seems like people can change a lot between lifetimes..." her voice trailed off as her mind drifted back to distant memories.

"What if I never stopped loving you?" Frank asked, gazing at her intently.

"Maybe love is the only thing that really lasts," Julia answered. "I guess I still love you too." Her eyes met his gaze and the world around them seemed to melt away.

At that moment nothing else seemed to matter. Ralph, Daniel, the housekeeping job, and her grandmother felt like distant memories. Abruptly, Julia found herself back in Jean Ferrier's house in Occitanie, longing for the touch of her kind benefactor. She felt a tremor run through her. It was just animal magnetism she told herself, but she knew there was much more. He wanted her and right now she couldn't think of a reason in the world to deny him. Daniel certainly wouldn't care, and to hell with him if he did. All he really seemed to care about was his stupid priest facade.

The memory of Daniel rushing away down the hall snapped her back to the present moment. She felt a deep stabbing in her heart, but she pushed it aside and gave Frank a come-hither glance. There was a strange fluttering in her heart as she stepped closer to him. His face and the face of Jean Ferrier shifted and merged into each other, and she loved them both.

Frank was breathing slow deep breaths. He reached out his arms pulling her to him. He had dreamed of this moment a thousand times, but he still wasn't ready for it. Dizzy and trembling he slipped his hands beneath her sweater savoring the smoothness of her skin, breathing in the scent of her. Letting her take the lead, he waited for the moment when she would ask for more. He kissed her lips, her neck, her cheek, until her mouth, hot and demanding, would not let him stray.

Quickly, so as not to shift the mood, he reached behind him to turn off the stove, then lifted her and carried her to the living room. A crackling fire made the room glow golden. Being so close to Julia made him ache with desire, her warm breath steaming in his ear, her hands stroking the muscles of his back with passionate concentration. She pulled him down to the floor. Then she was on top of him, pulling off his shirt and her own sweater. Her tongue traced the top of his shoulder and up the side of his neck.

"Julia," he whispered, breathless, "are you a virgin?"

"Umm," she moaned as he slipped his hand over her hips. "Yeah. Why?"

He felt a heady sense of joy. "I wanted to be the first."

Julia snuggled against him like a purring cat, her amber eyes glowing in the firelight. She wanted him to enjoy her body as she enjoyed it, lithe and sensuous. All this felt strangely familiar to her, the way her body felt in his arms, the sensation of his skin gliding over hers. Her virgin body yielded to Frank's embrace, but her mind was full of visions of Jean Ferrier.

Then she remembered nights under the full moon with her Romani lover, the musty smells of leaves and crushed grass and arousal hanging heavy in the air, and there was honeysuckle — always honeysuckle. But then the grizzled face of Lord Blackney would appear. The sharp pain of his entry made her cry out even now — or was it Frank? Ah, Frank? Where was Frank? Or was it Jean Ferrier? She was swimming in time. Revulsion and longing twisted into one another as she felt herself surrender to some irrepressible desire.

Again Lord Blackney loomed over her, and she remembered the words of spells that she had once repeated silently with all the power she could muster. Julia groaned, her heart feeling like it would break.

Frank's face reappeared, full of longing. "Kiss me," she moaned. Then in a whisper, "Do you really love me?"

Her lips ached for the touch of love and Frank kissed her, but suddenly she realized his love wasn't enough. She turned her head away. And it was Daniel's eyes she saw. Daniel, who had never held her, yet she felt the power of his love flowing through her like a flood. She forced him out of her mind.

"Julia," Frank hovered over her, gazing into her eyes. "I do love you."

She felt him claiming her body with a force she couldn't resist. "Frank. No, no I can't," she struggled against him even as she drank him in. Then she let go, helplessly sobbing as she climaxed.

Frank collapsed against her with a sigh. His arms felt safe and strong, but a vast aching emptiness yawned within Julia's heart.

Slowly at first, as if a tiny stream of water leaked in, the emptiness began to fill. She could almost taste it on her tongue, the sweet nectar of love.

Faster still she felt the stream rushing until it became a torrent of rapture. If only she could reach out far enough to touch him. She knew. It was Daniel. There was no doubt in her mind now. Only he could fill her with such ecstasy the way he, as Leo, had done so many times long ago.

She ran her hand through Frank's sandy hair, sadly thinking how easy it would be to pretend she loved him. And she did love him, of course. But it was like an echo of her former infatuation. She was not in love with him. Her heart belonged to Daniel. And she realized with a jolt that even if Jean Ferrier had become her lover in the past, her heart would always have belonged to Leo. In truth, it wasn't Ferrier's religion that had come between them at all. It was her love for another man.

She kissed Frank's cheek and nestled into the warmth of his arms as she drifted off to sleep. It seemed like only moments later when she awoke and looked around.

"Frank?" Julia's voice sounded harsh against the silence. It was dark now, and the fire had died down to embers. She was startled to find Frank gone. He had thrown a blanket over her and she sat up, pulling it tightly around her. "Frank?" She called again, more insistently.

"I'm right here, Julia." His voice surprised her with its nearness and she strained her eyes to find him in the dark. He was sitting in an overstuffed chair, not five feet away from her.

"What's wrong?" She sensed that he was brooding.

"I don't feel good about what we did — what I did." He spoke in a monotone. "You're only nineteen. I feel like I took advantage of you."

"We both wanted it, Frank. And anyway, age doesn't matter."

"Well, I'm old enough to know better. Shit, I'm practically old enough to be your father, Julia!"

"Barely." She shrugged with a practiced nonchalance. "We had to try it sooner or later, didn't we? The attraction wasn't just going to go away by itself. Besides, it doesn't have to change anything. We can still be friends."

"That's just it, Julia. I thought it *would* change things. I thought if we were lovers we could live together, you know, happily ever after, like in the movies." He bowed his head with a sigh. "But I could never be the one for you, even if I was younger, could I?"

Julia paused to consider his feelings before answering. "No, I guess not." She peered up at him, catching the glint of his eyes in the dark. "But you're the best friend I have. Maybe the only friend."

"All the more reason why I shouldn't take advantage of you," he answered morosely.

"Come on, Frank. Live and learn. There's no harm done. And it was, well, pretty amazing, wasn't it?"

"Yeah it was," he smiled sheepishly, pulling himself to a stand. He threw a couple of logs on the fire and then lay down beside Julia on the carpet. She snuggled into his arms and sighed.

"Can I tell you something, Frank?" She sounded hesitant.

"Sure. Anything."

"It was really me that was taking advantage of you. I was feeling angry and rejected and I think I was using you to get even, or maybe just to distract myself. I did love you though. I mean, I do love you, just not that way. I mean," she paused in confusion, "I — I love someone else."

"Tom?"

"No, it isn't Tom. It's someone just as much out of reach, though."

"Because he doesn't love you?"

"No. He does love me, but he's a — a priest, so he doesn't think he should."

"What? Oh no!" Frank sat up abruptly as he put it all together in his mind. "You sure know how to pick 'em, don't you?" After a slight pause he added, "It's the guy we met at your grandmother's house, isn't it? I thought I noticed a little spark there."

"Yeah, Father Murphy."

"You call him Father?"

Julia laughed. "I usually don't call him anything. Father does sound weird, doesn't it?"

Frank ignored her question. "So what? Are you just going to be his housekeeper and dream about screwing him?"

"Frank!" She protested. "You're so crude sometimes."

"Excuse me, but that doesn't sound like much of a life."

"I don't know what to do. And the worst part is that I hate priests. Not him personally, but I hate what priests did to me in the name of the church and what they did to people I loved. I still remember how they tormented me and burned the flesh off my bones, and I can still picture the jeering faces of the monks who tortured my lover to death. I see it all so clearly sometimes."

"Hmm — and there he is in the middle of all that. Ironic, isn't it?" Frank held her face between his hands and looked into her eyes. In the firelight his expression was clearly tender with concern. "Maybe that's why you picked him."

"No way!" Julia answered defiantly. "I didn't pick him. We were already connected. But he picked the church. Why didn't he pick me? We've loved each other for hundreds of years. He was the one they tortured to death. I can still hear his screams sometimes." She shuddered. "What could possibly have possessed him to become a priest after going through all that? I can't understand it."

"Like you said, people can change a lot between lifetimes," Frank offered.

Julia's eyes were fixed on the flickering glow of the fire. Even now she could envision the flames wrapping around her legs, searing her flesh. Frank pulled her close and she slowly drifted into dreams. His touch was very comforting.

CHAPTER 33

Breakfast

M orning dawned, bleak and gray. Julia stirred against the unfamiliar warmth of skin. For a moment she forgot where she was. Then her hand reached out to stroke Frank's arm. It would be the last time she ever slept with him, she thought. A tiny stab of remorse shot through her. Frank would have been a perfect partner in so many ways, but she wasn't in love with him. That would have made things too easy.

She sat up, gazing at Frank with appreciation. He was a good friend. That she knew. He opened his eyes and greeted her quizzically.

"Are you okay?" His eyes probed her face.

"Yeah," Julia smiled. "I was just enjoying being here with you."

"You don't feel bad about last night?"

"Not at all, Frank. I'll never regret it."

Frank thought for a moment and answered, "Neither will I, but I'm still sorry. I care too much about you to use you like that."

"Hey, love means never having to say you're sorry," she smirked. "Did you ever see that stupid movie? My mother used to quote it when I was little. She loved movie quotes."

"Sounds like bullshit to me."

Julia laughed. "Well, all I know is that I feel closer to you now, so maybe it was all for the best."

"Hmm," Frank mused. "Yeah, I feel closer to you too, Julia."

Together they stood up and began folding the blankets. On the carpet was a small bloodstain that had dried in the night. Julia noticed it first and blushed. Her memory was flooded with pictures of Lord Blackney's bed after the first time he raped her. She stood frozen, staring at the floor. Frank put his hand on her shoulder.

"Did I hurt you, Julia?" He spoke tentatively, pulling her close. "I wasn't even thinking about that."

She shook her head. "No." But something did hurt. Something inside of her ached for what she couldn't have.

She pulled on her clothes and went to the laundry room to find a cleaning solution. After a lot of scrubbing, she had removed most of the stain from the rug, but there would always be a slight trace of it. Frank said he liked it that way. It would remind him to be more considerate of people he cared about.

It was sobering to Julia, like a rite of passage. She had left her maidenhood behind which had begun with her first blood. With this blood she had entered womanhood. And if she ever bore a child, there would be another bleeding to mark her passage into motherhood.

It was something Frank wouldn't understand. To a man blood meant wounds, or war, or the hunt – different kinds of passages. She didn't try to explain what she felt. She simply put away the cleaning supplies.

It probably wouldn't even occur to Frank to remember that she carried his seed in her belly now. It could have been his child, if it had been a few days earlier in her cycle. A few days could make such a difference. No, he wasn't concerned with that. He was splitting logs to heat the house. Such a practical man.

Julia sat on Frank's corduroy-covered couch trying to imagine thousands of sperm swimming through her uterus. She felt invaded. She wanted them to die. Frank seemed so nonchalant about it. To him it was all over and done with.

She heaved herself to her feet and headed for the kitchen. It was a mess. Sautéed onions and peppers had crusted in the frying pan, forgotten in the heat of passion. Avocado, chilis and mushrooms had browned and withered on the chopping board. It would take some time to clean up.

While she worked, she could decide what to do about going back to her job at the priest's house.

The thought of running into Daniel Murphy made her queasy. On the other hand, she couldn't imagine walking away now that she was so sure of who he was. It felt like she had found her long-lost soul mate. He must feel it too. Maybe he even remembered being her lover all those centuries ago. Or perhaps he was just too confused to know what to think.

Of course she would have to go back, at least for a little while. It wouldn't be fair to leave the job without giving notice. That was the coward's way out. And waiting another day or two wouldn't make it any easier. In fact, the longer she put it off, the harder it would be. She was going to have to face the music — today.

Frank had finished splitting wood by the time Julia made her decision to go back to her job. He came in wiping sweat from his brow and looking famished.

"I don't know about you, Julia, but I could eat a horse — except I'm vegan," he laughed. "We forgot all about dinner last night."

"Well," she grinned as she wiped off the final countertop, "I just tossed your dinner in the compost bucket." She looked quizzically at Frank. "How long have you been vegan?"

"I went vegetarian when I was fifteen, after I saw my neighbors slaughter the two goats they had raised from babies. It was gruesome. I can still hear their screams. Since then, I've never been able to look at meat without thinking of that.

"Then I got the job at the dairy about a year ago and I saw how much suffering that industry caused — cows bellowing all night for their stolen babies and wailing newborn calves chained to veal crates waiting to be slaughtered. I couldn't eat dairy products anymore, so I figured I may as well skip the eggs too." He shrugged as if it should be obvious. "Chickens may be the most abused animals of all, the way they cut their beaks off and cram them in those tiny cages and crowded barns. Anyway, it just sort of happened, but since then I've been feeling a lot healthier, plus it's a lot better for the environment, so it's a win all around."

"Interesting," Julia mused. "So how 'bout I make you some vegan breakfast?"

"Allow me!" Frank pulled an apron over his head, moving into the kitchen with assurance.

"Suit yourself," she grinned. "Let me know if I can help."

Frank skillfully whipped up a batch of pancake batter while Julia watched. It seemed like only moments before he presented her with a perfect stack of pancakes and warm maple syrup.

"Wow! You never told me you were such a cooking pro," she purred.

"A well kept secret," he winked. "I once had a gig at one of those roadside diners where the truckers stop. Pancakes were my specialty."

"Well, you are all full of surprises." She leaned back in her chair with satisfaction waiting for him to join her.

"Go ahead. Don't wait for me. It'll get cold."

Julia hadn't realized how hungry she was. She couldn't wait to get started. They were the most delicious pancakes she had ever tasted.

"I've decided I have to talk to Daniel," Julia said, as she wiped her mouth with a napkin. "Things are just too weird the way they are."

Frank turned to look at her pointedly. "Does he know anything? I mean, about all that past life stuff. Have you ever mentioned it to him?"

"I don't know what he remembers, if anything. We haven't talked at all, really." Julia stopped to savor a bite. "I suspect something jolted his memory yesterday when he took off out of there like a bat out of hell."

"You probably scared the crap out of him. Weren't you talking about murdering your uncle?"

Julia laughed. "Actually, I don't think that's what bothered him. He was right there with me when my uncle showed up. It was after Ralph left that he seemed to get freaked out. He had this look in his eyes, like something had just dawned on him. Something wonderful. But then," she frowned, "it was like a horrible realization came over him."

"He remembered his vows?"

"Probably." Julia paused for a long time, then she spoke very quietly. "Maybe he realized what a mistake he had made."

"Don't get your hopes up, Julia. Those guys are pretty well indoctrinated."

"But he's not one of them," her voice was passionate. "When he remembers what they did to him he'll hate them as much as I do."

"Julia," Frank sat down across from her at the table with his own stack of pancakes. He reached out and took hold of her hands, "What if he has chosen to be a priest so he can heal all that? Not consciously, but maybe something in him wanted to experience life from inside the belly of the beast. Like, what if he is trying to find some good in what he used to hate?"

"Geez! You sound like my dad. He was a shrink," she added, noticing Frank's uncomprehending gaze. "That's deep stuff."

"Well," Frank shrugged uncomfortably, "I tend to think about things a lot, like why people do what they do. It's not always what you see on the surface."

"I'll say!" Julia slapped her hand down on the table and got to her feet. "I guess I'll just have to ask him. I'd better not put it off any longer." She leaned and kissed Frank on the cheek. "Great breakfast. Thanks."

CHAPTER 34

Conversation

V ery quietly, Julia opened the front door of the priest's house. She peeked into the living room and found it unoccupied. That was a relief. On exploring further, she was pleased to discover that Daniel was gone. Father Rosini sat at the table in the kitchen. He glanced up from his newspaper as Julia walked in.

"How is your grandmother doing, Julia? I heard she was home from the hospital."

"She's okay. They want her to stay home, maybe a couple more weeks, but she seems to be feeling a lot better."

"Good." Father Rosini went back to his paper and Julia began tidying up the kitchen.

"You won't have to make lunch today. I'm leaving soon and Father Murphy won't be home until dinner time. Rosini spoke as if he was reading his lines from the newspaper.

"Well, I'll have to make an especially nice dinner then."

The priest didn't answer. He was absorbed in a particularly interesting article in the sports section. Julia rolled her eyes. The guy acted like a robot most of the time, but for some reason sports ignited his passion. Learning the latest football scores seemed like the most important part of his day.

Julia hummed to herself and thought about what she could make for dinner. It looked like she would have most of the day to herself. That would give her plenty of time to think, and she had a lot to think about. In the last few days it seemed like her world had flipped into a tailspin — yet again.

By the time Daniel Murphy showed up, Julia had finished making lasagna for dinner and was adding the final touches to her salad. When she heard the front door open her breath caught as she waited to find out who it was. A moment later Daniel sauntered into the kitchen, greeted her casually and headed for his room. Julia was disappointed. He had barely looked at her.

Five minutes later he returned and stood silently in the doorway. Julia glanced at him curiously with eyebrows raised.

"I'm sorry I ran out on ya like I did yesterday," he began. His sea-blue eyes seemed to penetrate her soul. "I noticed that ya went home early. Father Rosini thought ya weren't feelin' well. Is that really why you left?"

"No. I was just kind of confused and overwhelmed, but I'm okay. Not sick anyway." She felt a bit guilty knowing that she hadn't gone home at all.

"Well," he smiled slightly, "t'was one of the strangest days of me life. I felt like I was somewhere else — someone else, like we were all in another time and place." He paused with a frown. "Who was that fella, anyway? That Ralph? Did you call him uncle?"

"Yeah, he's my uncle." Julia studied Daniel's face as she spoke.

"I've never felt such a revulsion toward another human bein' in me life."

"I'm not surprised. You have known him before, and I did too. We were all together once in another time and place."

Daniel looked perplexed. "What are ya sayin'? We've all lived before?" His brogue was thicker than usual.

Julia took a deep breath. "Would you believe me if I told you that my uncle had you tortured to death a long time ago?" She bit her lip, wondering if she had said too much.

Daniel was silent. His eyes bored deeply into Julia's as he shook his head. "Is that what ya believe?"

"It's what I know," Julia stated firmly. "You died in my arms."

Daniel paled visibly. There was no doubt in Julia's tone. She believed what she was saying without question, but how could it be true? None of it fit with anything he had learned in all his years at Catholic school and the seminary. Yet the feeling of recognition had been so strong. In some inexplicable way he felt that he had known both Julia and Ralph before. That had to mean something.

"Julia," Daniel moved closer struggling to find the right words, "I don't know what ta think. None of this seems possible, but I'll be the first ta admit I don't know everything."

"And I probably know less, but I do know what I know." She spoke emphatically. "It may seem strange to you, but I've lived with these memories for a long time. And I've known who my uncle is for over a year now. That's why I don't live with him anymore. He was part of the Catholic Inquisition and he had me burned as a witch. I've remembered bits of it in my dreams since I was little. More recently I had to relive it over and over again when I was awake, in vivid detail."

"My Lord!" Daniel crossed himself unconsciously.

Julia's eyes narrowed as she watched him resort to the familiar Catholic blessing. He has a lot to learn, she thought. Lord Blackney had only been one small part of the picture. There had been hundreds like him, monks and priests and noblemen who took pleasure in spreading terror and causing pain to others. Feeble characters individually, but powerful when aligned with the church. They fed on the agony and screams of their victims. Her lip curled and her eyes hardened.

"It's not over yet," she said. "The Inquisition may be gone, but human nature hasn't changed much. It could all happen again." Her vision was focused on something far away. "People don't want the truth. They'd rather see you burn."

Just then Daniel's cell phone rang. Julia watched through a fog as he answered it. After a moment he turned to her and held out the phone.

"It's yer grandmother," he spoke with a hint of relief. "She's wondering if I've seen ya. She says you haven't been answering your phone."

Julia took the phone with a quizzical frown. "Hi Grandma." She glanced at Daniel and then turned back to her salad, holding the phone between her ear and shoulder.

Carol spoke rapidly, wondering if Julia had seen Ralph and what had happened between them. She hadn't been able to get in touch with Ralph since yesterday and she was worried about him. After all, he had said something about a murder threat. Of course, she wasn't accusing Julia of anything. She was sure it was just a misunderstanding. Carol knew Julia better than to think she would murder anyone. Just the same she was concerned. Had they got into a fight? And why hadn't Julia come home last night? She was worried sick!

Daniel waited, trying not to listen as Julia explained that she hadn't seen Ralph since yesterday. He had run off before they had a chance to finish their conversation. And no, she hadn't stayed at the priest's house last night and it was none of Carol's business where she had gone.

Father Murphy was beginning to feel a bit awkward and he left the room just as Julia was saying goodbye.

"What a busybody!" Julia followed him and handed his phone back. "Why can't she mind her own business?"

Julia was more annoyed that Carol had interrupted her conversation with Daniel than with her snooping. He was finally beginning to communicate and her grandmother had to spoil it. He might never be so willing to talk again. After all, it wasn't every day that Ralph came around.

At dinner Daniel seemed to be brooding. Father Rosini asked him about changing the weekly Mass schedule, but Daniel just shrugged and said he wasn't bothered either way. His mind was somewhere else. He did take the trouble to tell Julia how good the dinner was. She appreciated that. Daniel seemed to look at her with a new respect. She wasn't just a housekeeper in his eyes anymore. In fact, she had become a compelling mystery.

Julia had lived with Ralph, Daniel mused to himself, probably feeling the same revulsion he felt, but not knowing why. Then one day she remembered. Could it be true, he wondered? Or was she insane? But if she was crazy, then how could he explain his own intense revulsion toward Ralph? Was he just tuning in to Julia's extreme hatred?

Even before he met Ralph, Julia herself had triggered a strong reaction, though it was positive in her case. She said he, Daniel, had died in her arms. Was that all? But even that was beyond his comprehension. He didn't believe in reincarnation. That was for Hindus and Buddhists. Catholics had evolved beyond such primitive beliefs. And yet he felt in his heart that he had known her before — somewhere, somehow.

Maybe she had a history of mental illness. That was something he should look into before he took anything she said too seriously. He decided to have a little talk with Carol. He would make it seem like he was concerned about Julia's welfare. Well, he actually was concerned, but the question of his own sanity loomed even larger. He was having experiences that nothing had ever prepared him for.

CHAPTER 35

Carmen de la Rosa

C arol was flustered when Father Murphy came to visit. She had only been home from the hospital for a few days and she wasn't able to play the congenial hostess as well as she would have liked. All she could do was offer him a cup of coffee while she tried to suppress her coughing. Still, she appreciated his visit. He even brought her flowers.

It seemed like Father Murphy was mainly interested in Julia, though. He was beginning to notice that Julia was different. She said things that surprised him. He wondered if she had a history of delusions or mental illness. Carol was quick to reply.

"Julia has always been — unusual. I don't know how else to explain it. It gives me the willies, but I have to admit that she seems to know things just out of the blue. Her mother was the same way. As children they could both tell what people were thinking. They'd speak your thoughts right out loud and it could be quite embarrassing. Julia even seemed to know the future sometimes, but nobody took her seriously until she predicted her parent's death in the plane crash.

"Her predictions were often right, but she was just a kid. None of us really believed in all that psychic stuff, you know — except for her mother of course. But after the plane crash Julia never made predictions anymore. Not to me anyway. I never knew why. Maybe she was afraid they'd come true. But, truth be told, I really wasn't around her much after she moved in with Ralph."

"Ya never asked her how she knew about the plane crash?" Daniel seemed incredulous.

"Frankly, that sort of thing has always scared me. I thought it was the work of the devil. I was glad when all her psychic nonsense stopped."

"Apparently it hasn't stopped," Daniel answered. "She still has memories of being burned as a witch by yer son."

"Oh good heavens!" Carol pulled her sweater up around her neck. "Do we have to talk about this?"

"I need ta know, Carol. Has she ever said anything ta you about past lives?"

"It's not something I believe in," Carol protested. "She may have said things, but — well, she was just a little girl. She had such a vivid imagination, you know."

"What sort of things did she imagine? I'm very interested in this."

"I can see that you are." Carol stirred uncomfortably in her seat on the couch. "Actually, there is a whole diary she wrote before she ran away. Ralph read the whole thing. He said she called herself Carmen de la Rosa. Can you imagine where she got a name like that?"

Daniel felt as if a bolt of lightning had shot up through his spine. He barely heard Carol as she went on.

"She tells about how she was captured by the Inquisition and burned as a witch and how she lived with Gypsies and learned magic spells."

"They prefer to be called Romanies," Daniel interrupted.

"Alright, Romanies," Carol corrected herself and continued. "I haven't read it myself, you know. I wouldn't do that without her permission, but Ralph told me the whole story. Now he thinks she's out to get him, because he abused her in some past lifetime." She eyed the priest thoughtfully. "If you really want to know more, Ralph would probably let you read the diary for yourself. He would love to have someone else read it, especially you being a priest. He's a good Catholic you know. All this stuff about reincarnation bothers him as much as it does me."

"Thanks, but I'll let Julia tell me what she wants ta know. I feel a bit awkward even askin' ya all these questions without tellin' her."

Daniel left Carol's house feeling a mixture of exhaustion and excitement. When Carol had mentioned the name of Carmen de la Rosa he had remembered a face. It was a beautiful face framed by raven-black hair with dark tear-filled eyes looking down at him. Carmen was someone he knew. Someone he loved more than his own life. He would have died for her. He would be willing to die for her again and again.

In that fleeting moment he had recognized her as surely as he breathed. Now it seemed too strange to be real. Carmen, if she had lived at all, was someone who had died centuries ago. Yet she felt as real and alive as anyone he had ever known, even more so.

His mind was full of these jumbled thoughts as he entered the living room of his house. Julia was waiting for him. Daniel stopped in his tracks when he saw her. This was no meek girl. Her amber eyes were blazing.

"Do you want to tell me what you've been up to, or should I tell you?" Her voice confronted him abruptly.

"I've been talkin' with yer grandmother. I'm sorry I didn't tell ya first," he answered sheepishly.

"That would have been the polite thing to do. Or maybe you could have just talked to me instead of whispering about me behind my back."

"Julia, I know how it must look, but I had ta find out more about ya. I had ta make sure ya weren't," he glanced at her apprehensively, "crazy."

"So now what? Are you going to have me committed?" She stood with her hands on her hips, glaring at him.

"I know you're not crazy Julia. You're just unusually gifted."

"Oh! Is that what my grandmother told you? How flattering." Her voice mocked him. "Can't you believe your own senses? Don't you even trust yourself, *Father*?" She spoke the last word sarcastically. "You're supposed to be a leader, a good shepherd and all that. Do you have to talk to my grandmother every time you run into something the Catholic church didn't tell you about?"

"I said I'm sorry, Julia. I was goin' to tell ya. I'm just tryin' ta get me mind around it. This is all so new to me." His boyish features were twisted with confusion.

"Okay," her voice was softer, but still sarcastic. "What did she have to say?" She backed off and sat on the couch staring at him. Daniel walked over and sat beside her.

"She told me about yer parents and how ya predicted their plane crash. She also told me that yer uncle had read yer diary and that he told her the whole story — about someone named Carmen de la Rosa." He spoke very gently and Julia looked like she was about to cry. "When she said that name, Carmen, I remembered a face. It was you, wasn't it?" He searched her eyes with his.

Julia could only nod. Tears filled her eyes.

"I loved ya, Julia. I would have willingly died a thousand deaths far ya."

Now Julia was crying openly, tears streaming down her cheeks. Daniel put his arm around her and stroked her hair.

"I still love you. I loved ya the moment I met you." He wiped her face with his sleeve. "And I thought ya loved me, but I didn't know why."

"You wouldn't have believed me if I'd told you." Julia took a deep breath to stop her sobbing.

"No I probably wouldn't have — then. I can hardly believe it now, but I guess there are mysteries in life that I'll never be able to understand."

"I suppose so," she shrugged. "Thanks for talking about it anyway. I didn't think you ever would."

"I wouldn't have known what ta say until now." He smiled, gently pushing a strand of hair away from her eyes. He looked at her curiously. "Do ya remember what me name was? Who I was in that other life?"

Julia's face brightened. "You were wonderful. Your name was Leo and you were always there for me when I needed you."

"Leo? Is that all ya remember?"

"It's a long story, Daniel — long and tragic, but beautiful too. Do you really want to hear the whole thing?"

"Of course I do."

"How 'bout after dinner?"

"Yer on." Daniel patted her knee and rose abruptly. "I'll see ya then."

"Daniel," she called softly as he began to walk away. "I do still love you."

He smiled sadly and left the room. Julia sat there for a long time feeling very peaceful.

CHAPTER 36

Dreams

Trouble whispered through the dreams of Daniel Murphy. He had listened to Julia's story feeling as though it was all unfolding before him. Now he lay in bed tormented by what his heart knew, but his mind could not accept. If indeed it was all true then how did it fit into his present circumstances?

A split opened wide within his being. He felt torn in two as the lover and the priest struggled within him for dominance. At one moment the priest would rise up personifying duty and barring his path to joy. Then his passion would push forward with tantalizing allure, pulling him away from his only chance at eternal salvation.

At times the lover transported him to raptures so ecstatic that his ideas of heaven paled by comparison. But the priest would then step in, gazing sternly in silent disapproval. Daniel felt cursed and blessed at the same time, the curse so horrible that he dared not imagine its repercussions and the blessing so wondrous that nothing in heaven or on earth could tempt him to let go of it.

Julia had brought him to this pass, but she could not follow him into the heart of his struggle. To her there was no question, no dilemma. In Julia's view his priestly vows were a folly, a ludicrous compromise, a blind devotion to the established order. Her revulsion toward the church was so strong that she could only view his vows as a huge mistake born of confusion based on lies.

She was undivided. Her heart seemed to hold no doubts. Daniel envied her. Even her hatred of the church was pure and unsullied by questions. It was all so clear to her. She hated everything and everyone that reminded her of the terrible fate she had endured at the hands of the Inquisition. It was that simple. Her hatred included her uncle, the Catholic church in general, Dominican monks in particular and anything smacking of patriarchy.

And when she loved, her passion was undivided. Nothing could stand in the way of it. That was the impression Daniel had gathered as he listened to her past life story. Carmen de la Rosa was not one to compromise. Her personality felt so vivid to him even now. He could almost see her dancing around the fire in their Romani camp. Even Julia's description of the black mare, Sloe, triggered something in his memory. He knew that horse so well. He could picture her coal-black coat and intelligent eyes in his mind as clearly as if he had parted with her yesterday.

Julia had told her story with such clarity and depth as if she was in a trance watching it happen on a movie screen. She had seemed not to even notice Daniel as she described scene after scene of a life lost in time. He was transfixed. Her joys and sorrows became his own. Reincarnation had never seemed plausible to him before, but after listening to Julia's story it seemed like the only possibility that made sense.

When she spoke of Leo, Daniel had begun to remember little flashes of dreamlike memories. Dark eyes laughing over him. Warm lips lingering against his cheek. Passionate whispers in the dark. It wasn't just her imagination. He could see it too — for an instant. He could feel the intensity of longing between them and he gazed at Julia with a strange mixture of fascination and desire. At the same time he was fighting it with all the strength he could muster.

A war had broken out in the once calm interior of his being. This was nothing he had ever been prepared for. Now, as sleepless hours passed, he felt trapped with nowhere to turn. Impossible as it was to put Julia out of his mind, it was even more impossible to quit the priesthood. His vocation had become the core of his identity. In spite of what Julia thought, he knew that his sense of purpose was rooted in the priesthood. People trusted him. They sought him out for help and guidance. Yet now he felt as if his own source of guidance had abandoned him.

Perhaps, he mused, he could do the same sort of work somewhere else. Maybe he could find fulfillment as a psychologist or a teacher. But such thoughts left a hollow feeling in his gut. Nothing felt right. He couldn't turn to anyone else for answers. Father Rosini wouldn't understand, and he knew what Julia would say. To her the answer was simple. He knew she loved him, but at the same time she looked upon his decision to enter the priesthood with disdain. It was obvious, even though she didn't say it aloud.

Julia arrived at work the next morning feeling wary. Last night after she had recounted the story of Carmen de la Rosa she had felt very exposed and vulnerable. Daniel had been deeply moved; she could tell. He had looked at her compassionately, but with a new sort of distance. He said he had a lot to think about and went off to his room immediately after thanking her for the story.

This morning he arrived at breakfast with dark circles under his eyes and a frown creasing his forehead. Julia watched as he picked at his waffles. His mind seemed miles away. He glanced at her once with eyes blazing, but quickly looked back at his plate. Something had changed in him, no longer her spontaneous Romani lover. He was more complicated now, more intellectual. Perhaps his past life ordeal had broken his once-free spirit. Simple answers didn't seem so simple to him anymore. But then, she wasn't the same either. Their carefree nights beneath the moon were like memories from childhood, far away and hopelessly innocent. Nothing seemed that easy now.

Julia longed for the effortless flow of communication she had known with Leo. He had seemed able to read her mind. Whenever she needed his help he was there. He had sensed her deepest desires and fulfilled them. Now his focus was somewhere else, occupied with thoughts of duty — and of heaven and hell. It seemed as though the church had successfully claimed his soul through the torture of his body. That was one more grievance Julia could add to her list of reasons to hate the church. It had stolen the devotion of her one true love.

Three days went by as she watched Daniel passing through the kitchen or the living room while she was working. He rarely spoke to her. His face looked drawn and pale from lack of sleep and the lines had deepened between his eyebrows. Now and then she would look up and catch his gaze as he watched her from across the room. He would smile dejectedly and sigh, shaking his head.

Finally, on the fourth day Daniel approached her while she was dusting a bookshelf and he spoke to her directly.

"Julia, somethin' has ta change. Either I have ta leave or you do. I just cannot concentrate on anything else when you're around. I've tried, but..."

"You don't really want to," Julia broke in. "Why don't you just enjoy it? Some people would give anything to fall in love like this. You are in love, aren't you?"

"Well," he looked at her helplessly, "that's the problem. I love ya way too much. I can't think of anything else."

"That's bullshit! There's no such thing as loving someone too much." Her eyes flashed with fire. "If anything, you don't love me enough." She turned and walked into the kitchen.

"Julia?" Daniel followed her.

"I'm not going to leave until my grandmother is ready to come back to work. It should only be another week or two at most and then you'll be rid of me. Why don't you take a vacation? Maybe I'll be gone when you get back." She never turned to face him, but began roughly pulling vegetables out of the refrigerator to prepare a soup for dinner.

"Fine," he answered with exasperation.

But he didn't take a vacation. A week later he was still stewing in his dilemma and Julia was still making his dinners. In fact she went out of her way to make things nicer than ever. There were always fresh flowers on the kitchen table and on his bedroom dresser. A Romani shawl was thrown over the back of the living room couch. She put a honeysuckle potpourri in the bathroom. Occasionally she would even tie a Romani scarf around her head and don golden hoop earrings. Daniel never consciously noticed how many changes there were around the house, but he picked up her messages just the same.

CHAPTER 37

Moving In

❦

"You know, Frank, I'm about ready to give up on Daniel. It seems pretty hopeless, but I hate to see him throw his life away," Julia grumbled as she sat stroking the corduroy pile on Frank's couch.

Frank glanced over at her from the hearth where he had begun to stack kindling for a fire. "Shit, I would have given up on him a long time ago if I was you. He's into the priest thing this time around. Be patient. Maybe you can snag him next lifetime."

"Very funny," she reached out with her foot to give him a light kick in the rear. She could tell by his expression that he was making fun of her. "I'm serious, Frank."

"Well, it seems like you've done all you could, Julia. The rest is up to him."

"But look at him! He's totally miserable. Why would he want to live like that?"

Frank turned to face her. "You know you could make his life a whole lot easier. All you'd have to do is get out of his hair." He struck a match and tossed it into the fireplace watching as his kindling teepee burst into flames. "Quite frankly, I think you kind of enjoy his misery."

Julia looked insulted. "I'm trying to help him."

"Ah! Maybe you should explain that to him. After all, he probably thinks you were sent by the devil to tempt him."

"He's not that stupid!" She was indignant. "He just doesn't know

179

how to reconcile his love with what he thinks is his duty, you know, his vows and all that."

"Yeah," Frank wiped his hands on his jeans, focusing his full attention on her. "So, what are you gonna to do about it?"

"You think I should just walk away don't you?" She eyed him with a pout. After a long pause she added, "I wish I could."

Frank forced a sideways smile and bounced onto the couch beside her. He put his arm around her shoulders and kissed the top of her head. "You know, Julia," he spoke softly in her ear, "whatever you decide I'll be here. And," he grinned boyishly, "if you need any help roping this guy I'll do whatever I can."

Julia shook her head trying not to laugh. "You're a goofball, Frank."

"One more thing," he added. "You may as well move in here. After all, you've been sleeping here for what, two weeks now?"

"It seems longer than that. It's just so weird going back to my grandmother's now. She thinks I'm having an affair with somebody, but she can't imagine it could be with you."

"So?"

"So why not keep her guessing," Julia laughed. "I may as well move in. But Frank," she gazed at him intently, "you have to promise to let me know if you ever want me to leave for any reason. Okay?"

"Sure," he shrugged.

"I'm serious. I don't want you to start resenting me."

"I don't see how I ever could, Julia. You're like the only kid sister I've ever had — sort of."

It was settled. Julia moved her few belongings into Frank's spare bedroom. Every morning Frank made breakfast and Julia washed the dishes. Every evening Julia came home to a warm fire and a friendly face. Sometimes they would fall asleep together snuggled under a blanket in front of the fireplace. Other times she would lie awake all night alone in her bed with thoughts of Daniel making her head throb.

Daniel had become her addiction. Like a drug, he got her high when he blessed her with his glance. She went through withdrawals when he didn't pay attention to her. Still, she treated him with cool reserve and lavished his house with her ardor. Bit by bit she would weave her web around him until one day he would realize there was no escape. That was her plan.

She thought about him that way when she was in a frenzy of despair. If he wasn't paying attention to her she plotted ways to ensnare him. But on those increasingly rare occasions when he greeted her with genuine affection all that dropped away. She was content to simply be in his presence.

When he heard that Julia had moved into Frank's house Daniel reacted almost imperceptibly. One stony glance into her eyes spoke more than any words could have said. But oddly enough, he relaxed a little. It became easier for him to laugh and joke with her. However, Julia wasn't fooled. In spite of his apparent relief he rarely let his eyes meet hers. He didn't want his jealousy to show.

Frank now had everything just the way he wanted. Well, just about. There was the problem of women, or the lack of a special one to be more accurate. He wasn't the kind of guy who expected to be celibate forever and now that Julia was living with him it was going to be awkward trying to get to know somebody else. Most women weren't too keen on their boyfriends having female roommates, especially young attractive ones. But for the moment it was perfect.

Living with Julia was much like he had imagined it would be. He adored her. She was like family. Her passions and dilemmas amused him, but he knew how important they were to her and he did his best to understand. This thing with Daniel Murphy worried him, though. She was letting herself get way too attached to the guy.

Reincarnation or not, people changed. Daniel wasn't the same person she remembered him to be. But then she seemed to know people pretty well. She could often read their thoughts so she must have some sense about Daniel. She must know that he really did love her or she wouldn't hang on the way she did. Even so, there was something very strange about it.

All Frank could do was watch from the sidelines. He watched as she came home with the news that Father Rosini was being transferred to a bigger parish and it was uncertain whether Daniel would stay on or not. Apparently the priests didn't have much say in the matter. They just went where they were told to go.

That put Julia into a tizzy. If Daniel was transferred to another parish she couldn't just go along as his housekeeper. In fact she wouldn't be able to go along at all. That thought made her sullen for several days.

Then one day she came home all bright and giggling. Daniel had been requested to stay until the new pastor arrived. It would only be a matter of a couple of weeks, but Daniel would be running the parish. He had been there long enough to become familiar with all the aspects of parish business. In all probability he would then be asked to stay on as assistant pastor. Frank could imagine her relief, but he would have preferred that Daniel was sent somewhere far away. Julia's preoccupation with the priest was becoming pathological in his estimation.

CHAPTER 38

Remembering

Daniel was much busier now than he had ever been since Julia met him. Father Rosini had been gone for two days and all the burdens of parish scheduling and finances had fallen on Daniel like a ton of cement. Julia did her best to make the transition smooth. Meals were served like clockwork and the house was cleaner than ever. Still, she got the feeling that Daniel resented her presence.

"I'll leave if you want me to," she blurted out suddenly as she set a tureen of lentil soup and a basket of sliced sourdough bread on the table one evening.

Daniel looked up at her, almost sadly, his aquamarine eyes glazed with confusion. "Why now Julia? Ya told me you wouldn't leave when I asked ya to before." His voice was quiet, without any fight in it.

"Now I think you really want me to go. My presence seems to bother you."

"Everything bothers me at the moment," he answered, heaving a sigh. "Sit down with me will ya?"

Julia sat across from him at the table, eyeing him curiously.

"What do ya want from me Julia? I feel like yer waitin' for somethin' ta change." Daniel looked straight into her eyes.

"I want the truth. That's all."

"Truth?" He repeated the word quizzically.

"Yeah truth. Like expressing what you really think and feel instead of always showing me this stony facade you walk around behind."

"Julia, what I think and feel is so confusing. I don't know that I could express it even if I tried."

"And it just keeps getting worse, doesn't it?"

"Yeah, it does. So?"

"So get a clue. Can't you see what you're doing to yourself? The more you pretend to have answers and the more you pretend not to feel anything the more confused you get, because you're denying the truth about what you really want and what you really feel." Julia looked exasperated. "Geez Daniel, your whole life is devoted to a religion based on St. Paul's mid-life crisis. You think it will get you into some sort of heaven when you die, but look at you. You've created hell in the here and now. That's not going to change just because you die."

"Ya don't know that."

"Oh yes I do. It may be the only thing I do know for sure. I've been there Daniel. I remember dying and look where I am now. And I remember watching you die. Does this look like heaven to you?"

"Good lord," Daniel groaned, clapping his hands to his head. This wasn't what he wanted to hear.

Julia continued. "Nothing is going to change unless you change it. This hell you're living in will follow you even beyond the grave. Believe me. I know." She gave him a piercing look. "Think about it Daniel. How long do you want to go on like this?"

"Okay!" He held up his hands to stop her. "You win Julia. There is somethin' very wrong with the way I've been handlin' things, but I'm not sure you have a better way."

"I didn't say I did. All I have is truth. I can only share what I honestly think and feel. The rest will take care of itself."

"Maybe so." He shrugged with an air of defeat.

"Look Daniel, I'm not asking you to marry me. I'm not even asking you to break any vows. All I want is what belongs to me. I can tell you feel love, but you're not sharing it. You're not letting it out and that is what's poisoning your whole existence."

Daniel's eyes met hers with a sudden flash of anguish. "I don't know how ta share it with ya, Julia. I'll be glad ta admit that I love you, but that's all I can do."

"Why isn't that enough?" She spoke softly.

"Is it enough?" He searched her face.

It felt as though her eyes enveloped him. Strange how they grew so dark and mysterious as he watched. Almost as if they were someone else's eyes. And now her whole face seemed to change.

"Julia?" His voice questioned the very reality of her presence.

She seemed to waver as far-distant memories rose up inside of him. Subtle sounds and smells surrounded him, growing stronger and pulling him into another time and place. Tin pots clanking, horses snorting, the aroma of stew simmering over an open fire. And she was there — the one with dark eyes and a smile that electrified him. The one he loved more than his own life. She was calling to him with her eyes, so sure that he would come. He couldn't refuse her.

"Carmen?" The wonder in his voice pulled Julia into his trance.

They both felt what they had shared so long ago. Time dissolved. Past and present blended. The fact that their bodies were different made no difference. It was only their souls that mattered. In some strange way it felt as if nothing had changed in hundreds of years.

The ever-widening chasm in Daniel's psyche snapped shut as a sense of oneness flooded over him. His internal war resolved. Rapture flooded in to fill the hollows in his aching soul.

"Carmen? What have I done?" He gasped the words, never taking his eyes from hers.

Her hands reached out to grasp his with a passion that seared through him. That touch ignited a fire of longing that erased all the weeks of anguish he had endured. He stood up and pulled her into his arms, drinking in the taste of her lips and the scent of her hair.

"Wait!" Julia pushed him back and looked deeply into his eyes. "Are you sure this is what you really want? If you regret it later it will only make things worse."

"It's what I choose now," he answered. "I know I'll never regret it."

Slowly and tenderly he began to caress every inch of her skin, pulling her clothes away like so much ethereal gauze. He was awash with memories now. The passion of a young Romani lad in the first flush of manhood rose up within him. A swelling belly ripe with child flashed before his eyes as he stroked Julia's softly curved waist.

"Yer belly was round with child when I loved ya before," he breathed in her ear.

"Then you do remember." Julia smiled, letting her body go limp against his chest.

He touched her just the way she longed to be touched, the way Leo had touched her. "Was the child mine?"

"I wish it was, but no. It was Blacknee's."

Daniel kissed her again. In one moment a gap of centuries vanished. Leo and Carmen rose triumphant from the ashes of their past filled with a fire so hot it consumed even time. As once they loved beneath a rising moon in a woods so distant that neither of them remembered where it was, they now lay in Daniel Murphy's bed, behind his locked door. White curtains billowed in the breeze and the scent of honeysuckle filled the air.

"Julia?" Daniel's voice softly broke the silence of the morning.

She looked like an angel bathed in heavenly light as the first rays of sunshine caressed her face. Flaming hair fanned out on her pillow like a glowing aura around her face. Her expression was one of pure serenity. He had never seen her look so beautiful.

Julia's eyelids fluttered open. The gold in her eyes flashed in the sunlight.

"Daniel?" Dimly she remembered where she was and a slow smile spread across her face. Hesitant at first, she searched his eyes, but found no regret there, no blame. He looked so boyish as he gazed down at her propped on one elbow with tousled hair and the lines of worry erased from his face.

For a long time they lay gazing at each other, listening to the silence and the first songs of waking birds. A whole universe seemed to unfold within the meeting of their hearts. Then slowly and deliberately they touched, choosing in that moment to embrace each other as they were now. No memories swept them back to forgotten moments in the past. Their lips met as if for the first time giving rise to rapturous communion. Suspended without breath, hearts pounding, they seemed to float outside of time. Rising on waves of rapture they merged, balanced on the peak of ecstasy, collapsing in exquisite surrender washed clean of all desire. Waves of bliss flowed back and forth between them like a tide as they lay bathed in peace.

"I would have been a fool ta let ya go, Julia," Daniel sighed, kissing her fingertips.

"I know," she smiled smugly. "But you will have to let me go eventually if you really want to be a priest."

"I suppose," he pulled her close against him with a moan, "but I don't want ta think about that right now. This is the first time I've had a moment of peace since I met you."

Julia grinned. "You fought it awfully hard." Her face softened as she looked into his eyes. "You won't be sorry later will you?"

He shook his head. "I'll never be sorry, Julia. Right now I belong here in yer arms. Tomorrow may be different, but even so I'll never regret what we've shared. It's a treasure I will always carry with me, just like the memories we have of our past lives."

"I'm glad."

"No matter what happens," Daniel fixed his gaze intently on her face, "don't ever forget that I love ya. I always will." He closed his eyes and lay back on his pillow. "I'll never forget."

"I know, Daniel. I just wanted you to acknowledge the truth. You would have killed yourself the way you were trying to bottle it up inside."

"Yer right about that. It probably would have killed me sooner or later." He exhaled with relief, lost in his own thoughts.

"It's not about sex you know," Julia murmured as she ran her fingers over the muscles of his upper arm.

"What isn't?" Daniel frowned slightly.

"Any of this. We don't need sex to be where we are now."

Daniel's frown deepened, but he knew the truth of what she was saying. He had felt just as close to her in the weeks before, but he had refused to accept it. The last time he had let himself feel her so deeply he had been flooded with confusion. Such bliss wasn't meant for this world — and certainly not for priests.

"That's what you were thinking about isn't it?" She prodded.

"Yeah. It's that age-old question. How can I reconcile romantic love with the priesthood?"

"Well, not exactly age old. More like a few centuries. The church hasn't even been around for ages," Julia teased. "Anyway, you'll always know what's right when you trust your heart. Just be true to yourself and ignore what anyone else tells you. Margaret Littlewolf, the old Native American woman I met when I was living in the woods, taught me that."

"This?" Daniel waved his hand over them with a bemused smile. "Lyin' here naked with a beautiful woman after havin' taken a vow of celibacy? I've spent the night makin' love and enjoyin' the hell out of it," he laughed. "But I would never have thought it could be right before."

"And now?"

"Now? I can't think of any time I've felt more at peace — or more holy in the sense of wholeness. I actually feel whole for the first time in me life."

"Even though you're breaking your vow?" She asked with sincere concern.

"I've realized somethin' about vows, Julia. And I have you ta thank for it. Vows are choices that we make in one moment as a way to lock ourselves into a pattern that we think is best for us at the time. But they don't allow for growth or new realizations. We take vows because we don't trust our future self. We don't trust the divine spark inside of us. We're afraid that we won't be as wise at a later time, but if we're growing, we should actually be gettin' wiser as we get older.

"I've come to realize," he continued, "that the vows I took as a graduate from the seminary are not actually servin' who I am in this moment. Those vows were designed by the church to keep people like me under control. They were not somethin' I chose out of me own desire to live in celibacy. I only took the vows in order to be admitted to the priesthood, because I felt that my calling was to serve people through the church."

"So your vows mean nothing to you?"

"No. I wouldn't say that. It's hard ta explain, Julia. I wouldn't break them lightly. I understand the spirit of the vows and I intend ta follow them as guidelines in me life. But I'll also allow myself the freedom ta choose in each moment what is best fer me."

"From what I've read, the celibacy vow is all about passing the priest's property back to the church, rather than to any children he might have if he wasn't celibate. Hardly seems like there's much spirit in that."

"I suppose that could be true," Daniel answered with a slight frown. "But no matter. The God within me is my supreme authority. I won't put any other authority above it, not the church, not anyone. And right now I feel closer ta God than at almost any time in me life. And that's really all that's important."

Julia smiled, leaning her face on her hand as she looked down at him. "Reminds me of another thing Margaret said. She taught me pretty much everything I know that's of any value. She said there's nothing more important than honoring the Great Spirit inside of us. That's how we find our wholeness. And when we create division inside of ourselves we cut ourselves off from that life-giving force. Then we start to die. So, no matter what choices we face we can always listen to the Great Spirit and find the best answers that make us feel whole and energized. It works for me."

"So, you're sayin' that if I had just accepted the energized feelin' in the first place I would have saved meself a lot of anguish." He laughed. "Ya make it sound so simple."

"According to Margaret, life really is simple. Just do what makes you feel uplifted. Appreciate everything, even stuff you don't like, and enjoy life as much as you can. Then it just keeps getting better and better. She was a very wise and happy person."

"And what if bein' a priest makes me happy?"

"Then I guess that's what you should be doing. But," she frowned slightly, "not if you have to compromise your truth. If that really is what you want, then you have to find a way to follow your heart and still do what the church tells you, I suppose. Do you think being a priest is enough to make you happy for a lifetime?"

"I guess that's fer me ta discover. I do love being a priest." Their eyes met with clarity.

"Why?" Julia blurted the question without thinking. "How can you after what the church did to you in the past — what it did to both of us?"

"Maybe it has ta do with me parents," he answered after a pause. "They gave up a lot so I could go to the seminary. They're the most lovin' people I have ever known and they lived fer their Catholic faith. They still do."

"But that's not about you Daniel. How does it feed your soul?"

"It does somehow. I don't know if you could ever understand, Julia. It gives meaning to me life. I never thought about reincarnation at all until I met you, but it makes a lot of sense when I look at things that way now. Maybe on some level my soul realized that I would have ta forgive the church for the agony it inflicted on both of us. Maybe I'm tryin' ta find love where I could only hate before."

Julia gazed at him with tears in her eyes. "I couldn't do that, Daniel. I have so much hate for the church I don't think I could ever forgive." She felt humble, as though the nobility of his spirit far surpassed her own. She smiled sadly. "And I thought I had something to teach you."

"You've taught me a lot, Julia." Daniel pulled her head to his chest and kissed her hair. "A lot more than you'll ever realize."

"Well, I'm learning much more from you." She kissed his lips and then turned to get up.

"Don't do it fer the church." He said, casting an admiring glance at her as she stood by the bed. "Do it fer yerself. Do it to set yer soul free."

"Do what?"

"Forgive. Just fer your own inner peace. It won't make any difference to the church." Daniel sat up, swinging his legs to the floor.

Smiling to himself, he watched Julia walk naked into the hallway. They'd left her clothes lying on the kitchen floor.

CHAPTER 39

Invasion

⁊⁊

"We're not going to have much more time alone together," Daniel told Julia as he put down his phone. "The new pastor will be arrivin' day after tomorrow."

"Already?" Julia swallowed hard. "I guess that means the honeymoon's about over."

"We both knew it couldn't last long," Daniel put his arms around her and looked into her eyes.

"Yeah," she rested her head on his shoulder. "Anyway, my grandmother's a lot better now. She'll want her job back soon. Plus," she chuckled, "I'm getting tired of sneaking in and out of here after hours. I don't want to give all those parish busybodies anything to gossip about."

"Well let's not rush things. We can find somethin' fer you ta do around here when your grandmother comes back. You'll just have ta stay out of me bed."

Their eyes met in a mutual grin.

"I guess Frank must be wondering what happened to me," Julia mused, half to herself. "I haven't been home in three days."

Daniel's eyes narrowed. The mention of Frank sent a pang through him.

"What?" Julia looked at him with concern, feeling his angst.

"You weren't a virgin were ya?" His tone expressed little doubt. "I assumed that Frank was yer lover."

Julia winced. "I guess it must have looked that way, but we're really just friends." She glanced at Daniel to see his reaction. Then, after taking a deep breath she went on. "We did have sex once, but we both realized that it wasn't right." She paused, meeting Daniel's gaze. "Does that make you jealous?"

"Yeah it does," he admitted, "but I can't blame ya. It's not like I was available."

"Actually, I was so angry with you. It was my way of getting back at you for rejecting me. I wanted somebody just to want me, and Frank happened to be willing and able. Not the best reasons in the world, but no harm done. At least we can still be friends."

Just then a loud knock at the front door interrupted their conversation. Julia looked up, startled, as the intimate warmth between them turned cool. A formal public facade dropped into place with practiced smoothness. Frowning, Julia headed toward the front door. Something told her it was not a welcome visit. In fact, she had a feeling of foreboding so strong that it was all she could do to force herself forward. Danger waited outside that door.

She glanced back at Daniel with a frown, hesitating.

"What is it Julia?" He stepped forward sensing her fear. "Ya look like you've seen a ghost."

"I don't know, but it's not good," she whispered.

With trepidation she reached for the doorknob and turned it, pulling the door toward her. Everything seemed to be moving in slow motion. Daniel edged closer, wondering what could possibly be upsetting her so much. There in the doorway stood Ralph McCullen.

This time Ralph wasn't running with his tail between his legs. He was angry. Angry and reeking of booze. In his hand the gleaming blade of a butcher knife flashed in the sunlight — the knife Julia had dropped on his bedroom floor. His eyes were wide and crazed.

"Now I've found you, whore, witch!" Bellowing, Ralph staggered into the house, slamming the door behind him. "You were going to kill me with this, weren't you?" He yelled, brandishing the knife wildly in her direction. "Well, I'm not going to give you another chance." He laughed maliciously, then paused with a sneer. "You thought I'd never figure it out didn't you? You thought I'd never know it was you and your wicked curse that ruined my life. Thought you were so clever didn't you, little Carmen?" He suddenly noticed Daniel and faced him with a jerk. "You want to know what she did to me, Father?" I can see you're dying to know. She could do it to you too if you weren't careful. Not that you should care," he muttered under his breath. Then his voice boomed, "She's a witch you know!"

"Leave him alone, Ralph. This is between you and me." Julia faced him with all the courage she could muster.

"Okay bitch. I'll settle it once and for all." He swung the knife blade wildly grazing her cheek with its sharp tip.

Daniel leapt into action grabbing Ralph by the elbows and pinning his arms behind his back. The knife flew to the floor. Julia clapped her hand to her cheek and pulled it away gasping as she watched drops of blood drip onto the flowered carpet. Rage surged within her, erasing every whisper of fear.

"You cursed me you she-devil! I read it in your diary." Ralph was yelling again and struggling to escape from Daniel's grip.

Suddenly Julia had an idea. A slow eerie smile spread across her bleeding face. What if Carmen's curse had worked?

"Ha! I know why you could never marry," she mocked him with a malicious grin, "and why that woman left you, the one you were engaged to. You always blamed it on Grandma, but it wasn't Grandma's fault was it? She didn't scare that woman away. It was all you!" Julia paused as Ralph struggled even harder. "I bet you're totally impotent and it drives you crazy, because you're obsessed with sex. That woman found out your secret didn't she? Isn't that why she left you?"

"Shut up you slut," Ralph yelled. It was everything Daniel could do to hold him back.

"You thought you could escape my curse by joining the seminary and becoming a priest, didn't you Ralph? But it only took them a few months to catch you with your pornography and they kicked you out. Right? Isn't that what happened?"

Julia went on with a vengeance. "You thought taking a vow of celibacy could save you. Ha! But even priests get horny, don't they Daniel?" She glanced at her lover with an amused smirk. "Taking a vow can't fix that," she jeered. "It definitely wouldn't work for you, Uncle Ralph. I bet the hornier you got the more you tried to suppress it, and that made it even worse. And now all you can feel is the burn of unfulfilled desire, which is exactly what you deserve — to burn just like you burned me!" She stepped closer. "I hope you've learned your lesson Ralph. I hope you've learned that it's not okay to burn people alive or torture them to death. And it's not okay to rape people, even if you did pay good money for them. It's not okay at all," she screamed in his face.

"Damn you!" Ralph lashed out with a sudden burst of energy breaking free of Daniel's grasp. "That wasn't me! You're out of your mind Julia!" With a wild screech he leapt at Julia gripping her neck with a strangling force. "It wasn't me! It wasn't me!" He shouted in her ear as his hands crushed her throat.

Daniel reacted with superhuman speed grabbing Ralph by the shoulders and flinging him across the room. He watched in horror as Ralph's body hurled headlong against the coffee table, its sharp corner gashing his temple as he collapsed into it. Ralph lay limp, twitching occasionally as blood oozed out over one pink flower of carpet pile.

Aghast, Daniel stood frozen and pale as he realized what he had done.

"Oh my God! I've killed him!"

"He's still breathing," Julia choked, clutching her neck as she rushed to Ralph's side. "Maybe he'll be alright."

"I'll call an ambulance." Daniel left the room abruptly.

Julia could hear his panic-stricken voice giving directions over the phone. There wasn't much she could do for Ralph. He didn't seem to be conscious, but his breath was steady. Now and then a spasm twitched through his body. Then he lay so still that Julia held her breath praying that he would move again.

As she gazed down at Ralph's limp body a sudden realization washed over her. The words of Margaret Littlewolf echoed in her mind, "It's all just your own reflection." Julia felt tears rush to her eyes and she began to sob.

"Do I really have that much hate and anger inside me?" She saw it so clearly now. It was a burden she had carried with her all her life, so familiar that it felt like a part of her.

Ralph looked so helpless, crumpled and harmless with his mouth wide open, his pale face haloed by a small pool of blood. He was right. It wasn't him anymore. Lord Blackney may have been a part of him way back in the Middle Ages, but it really wasn't fair of her to hate Ralph now. He had never done her any harm in this lifetime — at least not until she scared him into it. She put her hand over his heart, relieved to feel it beating softly.

"I'm sorry Uncle Ralph," she whispered, more to herself than to him. "My memories seemed so real, but you're right. Blackney wasn't you. You are a new person now, just like I am."

Daniel walked in as she leaned to kiss Ralph's forehead. He smiled sadly.

"I hated him too, Julia. I had a horrible feeling the moment I heard his voice. I sensed that you were right about what he did to both of us a long time ago, but I didn't want...," he broke off as tears filled his eyes. "It was hatred that made me throw him so hard."

The sound of approaching sirens whined in the distance. Julia looked up at Daniel and their eyes locked in full realization of the impact of the moment. Everything would be different from now on.

"Please don't blame yourself, Daniel. It was really all my fault. I'm so sorry I got you involved in this." She bowed her head, tears streaming down her face. "You should have just let him strangle me. I would have deserved it."

"Julia," Daniel knelt by her side as she slumped to the floor beside Ralph's motionless body, "the man came here threatening ta kill ya. He had a knife in his hand."

"But I egged him on. I was trying to infuriate him. I knew just what to say to piss him off. But," she turned to Daniel and burst into renewed tears, "I didn't want this to happen."

Sirens were now blaring outside the house. Daniel kissed Julia on the cheek and helped her to her feet. Together they opened the front door to meet the ambulance crew. Two cops followed the paramedics into the house. "We got a report of a home invasion and attempted murder. I need to get statements from both of you," the older of the officers told them as he took a quick survey of the room. "Was this a forced entry?"

"Hold on," Daniel put them off. "Let's get him ta the hospital first. We'll have plenty of time to tell ya all the details once he's in the ambulance." He scanned the faces of the paramedics for signs of hope as Ralph was lifted onto a stretcher. They looked grim and professional.

"Is he going to be okay?" Julia asked.

"We'll do the best we can," a young woman in pale blue scrubs answered.

As Ralph was carried to the ambulance, Julia and Daniel followed and watched as the paramedics hooked him up to oxygen and a heart monitor. He looked as innocent as a child. The ambulance doors closed and the vehicle sped off toward the hospital with its siren shrieking. Julia and Daniel turned to discover a small crowd of bystanders gathered around the scene. Curious eyes followed as they walked back to the house with their arms around each other. One pair of eyes belonged to Frank Davis.

"Julia!" Frank called out as he pushed through the crowd. He caught up to her just as she entered the house.

"Frank! What are you doing here?" She gave him an exhausted hug.

"I happened to be driving by and I wondered what all the commotion was about. That looked like your uncle on the stretcher." He drew back suddenly to look at her. "You're bleeding! What the hell happened here?"

"It's not that bad," she answered, gently touching the cut on her cheek. Ralph came at me with a knife."

"Holy shit!" Frank exclaimed then stopped himself, awkwardly glancing at Daniel. "Sorry Father." He turned back to Julia. "Then why is he the one in the ambulance?"

"Daniel stopped him, and Ralph fell and hit his head. It was a total accident."

"Geez!" Frank looked at Daniel with a new respect. "He probably saved your life."

"Yeah. Maybe he did. I think Ralph was drunk enough to try anything."

CHAPTER 40

Release

⋙⋘

For two days Julia sat at Ralph's bedside feeling guilty. There were times when her grandmother joined her for a few hours and times when Daniel sat with her, riddled with remorse. Frank stopped by in the evenings after he got off work at his construction job. Mostly though, she sat alone reflecting and trying to understand.

She didn't want Ralph to die. Even when she had written about strangling him in her diary, it was just a flare of temper. She had never really wanted to hurt him physically. And now she swore to herself that if he lived she would take care of him for the rest of his life. She felt she owed him that much after driving him to the snapping point that led to his injury. The doctors told her he might recover fully, but he might also remain in a vegetative state indefinitely. There was certainly brain damage, but they couldn't tell how extensive it was yet.

It was impossible for Julia to hate a man who looked so utterly defeated. Hate, she supposed, was just another face of fear, and his crumpled body no longer triggered her fear. She could only feel sorry for him.

His presence had sometimes felt threatening to her in the past, but now she realized she had never really allowed herself to see him at all — not the man he was now. She had confused him with a man who lived hundreds of years ago. That was another part of him perhaps, but he wasn't the same man anymore.

Now he looked as helpless and harmless as a baby. He lay in a coma unaware of time, floating off somewhere far away where nobody could reach him. Still, Julia talked to him. She had read somewhere that people could still hear even when they were unconscious. Maybe he was listening.

As she talked, all her feelings of revulsion and hatred came up again. She told him how hard it was to live with the memories of his past-life cruelty, how those memories had tormented her more and more as her visions became more vivid.

"You know, Ralph," Julia told him, "there were times when I thought I'd feel some satisfaction in hurting you, but even then I could never have done it. And I know it wouldn't have made me feel any better, because all I really wanted was for you to see me and respect me – the real me. Not me as your niece or your wife or your property. I wanted you to see my soul that seems to be connected with yours in some twisted way." Tears rolled slowly down her face catching on the scab from the knife cut on her cheek and running down its length.

"I wanted you to recognize that I am a valuable person," she continued, "worthy of your esteem and love. Someone you could never dream of raping, or burning at the stake, or hurting the way you hurt me in the past. But I guess I didn't treat you with much respect, either. Maybe you wanted the same thing from me, otherwise you wouldn't have been so angry when you read my diary and saw how much I hated you.

"I always thought you were weird, even when I was a kid. You actually scared me, but for a long time I didn't know why. You had so many quirky habits and you seemed so weak, but also dangerous. I remember my father saying things about you when I was little. He made it sound like you had severe emotional problems. I didn't realize then that he spoke with compassion when he said those things. He wasn't blaming you.

"I always wanted to blame you. I guess I was born with a grudge against you. And maybe my curse really did affect you somehow. I don't know. I don't even remember what it was except that I spat on you with a lot of hate just before I was burned." Julia wiped a tear from the corner of her mouth. "All that stuff I said when you came at me with the knife was made up on the spot just to piss you off. I knew you were so drunk you'd believe anything." She paused for a moment watching his impassive face. "I'm so sorry. I'm really, really sorry.

"My friend Margaret Littlewolf used to tell me that it's all my own reflection, everything I experience — you, Grandma, this hospital, the church, everything. It's all reflecting my own beliefs and expectations back to me. And if I can't accept what is, it's only because I don't accept myself enough. I've been thinking about that a lot lately.

"Margaret also told me that we get whatever we focus on. So it doesn't make sense to blame other people for anything, 'cause it's just our own beliefs that shape our experience in the first place. That's been hard to accept, but I'm beginning to get it. Like when I was just paying attention to your faults, I could only believe the worst about you. Maybe if I had tried to appreciate the good things about you, I would have been able to see your best side and none of this would have happened. I'm sure there must have been good things that I never even noticed, maybe a lot of good things.

"I guess it all comes down to love. If we love someone we notice more of the good things about them. I was pretty much doing the opposite with you.

"Anyway, I think I'm finally ready to let go of the past. I'm going to try, at least. I really don't want to hate you anymore. I don't want to hate anyone, so I'm choosing to forgive you. It's not easy, but I have to do it, and I hope you will forgive me for all the pain I've caused you.

"I've realized through all this that I actually do love you Uncle Ralph, in my own mixed up way. They say you can only hate someone you love. Otherwise you wouldn't even care, so I guess I loved you all along, but it got twisted up with pain." She let out a deep sigh.

"That's another thing Margaret used to talk about. There really is only love, ultimately. Hate is just love turned backwards through pain and misunderstanding. I got caught up in the backwards version of it." Julia laughed sarcastically. "I'm learning, slowly."

Suddenly reality wavered and Julia felt herself being sucked through a dark tunnel. With a pop, she found herself in another room, or maybe it was a garden. There were thriving plants all around her, but also windows and open doors through which she could see wide vistas of rolling hills, glittering cities, charming woodlands and ocean beaches. There was no ceiling and she could see puffy white clouds drifting across the blue sky above.

"Is this the afterlife?" Julia asked aloud.

"It's my life," Ralph answered. "Or an aspect of my experience."

Julia turned to see Ralph standing behind her, looking as he had in his youth and yet somehow even better. His thick red hair was tousled in the breeze and his blue eyes sparkled more than Julia had ever thought they could.

"How did I get here?" Julia asked in wonder as she turned to take in all the views around her. "It is so beautiful."

"You asked for it. You wanted us to see each other as we really are — and you know wishes always come true."

"Do they?" Julia sounded skeptical.

Ralph waited for her to think about it for a moment. "It takes time in the earthly dimension, but here everything happens instantaneously."

"Why were you so cruel to me as Lord Blackney?" Julia blurted out without thinking. "I never wished for that."

Ralph smiled sadly. "Don't you remember?"

Julia was suddenly flooded with memories from many centuries ago, back to a lifetime long before her life with Lord Blackney and she felt a jolt of electricity run up her spine. "Oh my God! You were my daughter in another life and I was a horrible father. I sold you into slavery for the money. I didn't care about you at all."

"And yet you did care. You cared enough to share lifetime after lifetime with me so we could finally come to this point," Ralph said.

One by one, a series of other lifetimes flashed through Julia's memory. "There was a life where you were my brother and I murdered you. And another life where you were my wife and we were constantly fighting."

"There were so many other lives. So many, where we hurt and mistreated each other, all so we could learn to recognize the truth," Ralph spoke gently.

"The truth? Julia looked at him with confusion. "You mean the truth that we are not so different from each other? That we have both been cruel?"

"Well, that, but also the truth that we were never really victims — neither of us. And the truth that love was the force that kept drawing us together. We always had the power to change our reality and remember the love, but we didn't use it."

"Like Dorothy in the Wizard of Oz," she mused. "Where Glinda says, 'You always had the power, my dear, you just had to learn it for yourself.'" Julia pondered the possibility that she might have avoided all the drama of her past if only she had kept her focus on finding the love in her present experience. Then she had a brilliant realization.

"In a way, I wanted all that drama. I wanted to experience persecution. I wanted to know what it felt like to be used and abused, because — that's how I could get in touch with my own power. I had to be pushed to my limit before I would finally stand up for myself and declare that I wasn't going to take it anymore. Never again!"

"Yes!" Ralph grinned at her. "Never again! And I was learning the same lesson right along with you. We were actors on a stage together, each playing our roles for the other."

"It's all going to be different now, isn't it?" Julia already knew the answer as she gazed at him with a new appreciation. "It's like we are graduating to the next level and it's going to be a lot more fun next time we meet."

"Definitely a lot more fun," Ralph agreed, laughing, and he began to fade away as if dancing into a mist like a swirl of vapor.

The world around Julia was wavering again and she felt herself being pulled back through the dark tunnel. Harsh lights assaulted her eyes as her awareness returned to the hospital room where Ralph's body lay imobile in the bed.

Ralph died that night with Julia and Daniel by his side. Julia was watching his face as he took his last breath. His eyes flashed open just for an instant and she could have sworn that he smiled at her, but that might have been wishful thinking. Even so, Julia felt that a huge burden was suddenly lifted from her soul. The hate that had riddled her life evaporated like fog in the sunshine. She felt as if she might never know joy again, but her sadness was filled with a new serenity.

Daniel had come to the hospital to perform the last sacrament before Ralph died. Julia imagined that Ralph would have wanted it that way. She watched humbly as her lover anointed the body of her uncle and prayed for his soul. Daniel really did take his role as a priest seriously. It almost seemed to make sense. Almost.

Together Daniel and Julia felt peace descend as Ralph's soul drifted through the veil between worlds. Daniel was solemn with the realization that he had inadvertently taken Ralph's life. He pulled the sheet over the dead man's face with grim finality. When he turned to look at Julia they both knew that their relationship would never be the same. Every time they met now the specter of Ralph McCullen's death would rise up to join them, blasting away any thoughts of romance.

They gazed at each other for a long time feeling the weight of the moment. This is the way love really feels, Julia thought to herself. There was no giddy rapturous emotion pulling her off balance. No unmet longing. It was simply the meeting of two people who knew each other as deeply as it was possible to know, because they had each opened their soul to the other.

There was no need for words. They each knew exactly what the other was feeling. Julia and Daniel would always have that connection, no matter what twists and turns the future might bring them. They would always find each other again.

Epilogue

Frank took Julia's hand as they walked toward his truck. A small group of church acquaintances had attended Ralph's burial and now they were dispersing, wandering solemnly through the cemetery.

"I'll drop by tomorrow after my job interview at the vet clinic," Julia told her grandmother as they got ready to leave. "My summer classes at the JC don't start until June, so I'll have plenty of time to visit. Maybe we could go out to lunch."

"I'd like that," Carol said wearily.

Julia gave her a questioning look of concern.

"I'll be okay, Julia." Carol smiled sadly. "By now I should be getting used to death, but it always takes the wind out of my sails for a while. It's just one of those things we have to deal with in life, but it does seem to get a little easier over time."

Julia pulled her into a long hug. "I'm here if you need me, Grandma. Just call. Anytime."

"I'm actually more worried about you, Julia. You've been through so much. Are you alright?"

Julia grinned. "You know, I never would have expected it, but I feel better than ever. I mean, it's like a huge weight has been lifted off me. I can finally breathe! I feel free for the first time in my life."

"I'm so glad to hear that." Carol smiled, stroking Julia's cheek. "I was afraid Ralph's death might push you over the edge."

"Been there, done that," Julia chuckled, remembering her flight to the forest. "No. I'm good. I'm really excited about getting into veterinary school and leaving the past behind. I might even get a dog, if it's okay with Frank — like a service dog puppy I can train. It feels like I have a new lease on life."

"That's wonderful. And I hope you will let me pay for your education. Heaven knows, I haven't been able to give you much. At least let me do that."

"Thanks Grandma. I'd really appreciate that."

"What's this about a dog?" Frank chimed in. "How would that work with school and a job?"

"If I'm training a service dog, I'd be allowed to take it with me. They can go anywhere. Not a problem."

"Hmm. I guess that could be fun. Why not?" Frank shrugged and grinned at Carol. "Julia is full of surprises."

"That she is," Carol agreed. "She'll keep us on our toes. You just make sure she doesn't go running off again. I'm depending on you for that."

Carol gave Frank a little squeeze and a pat on the back as she said goodbye. He's turned out to be a pretty good egg, she thought to herself as she walked toward her car.

Daniel Murphy had been watching as he stood beside the open grave. In spite of his remorse, he felt blessed by Ralph's death. It had freed him from his recent confusion and doubt.

Since Carol had returned to her job as housekeeper, Daniel wouldn't be seeing Julia so often anymore. He suspected that Ralph's funeral might be the last Catholic function Julia would ever attend, at least until her grandmother passed away, and that probably wouldn't happen anytime soon.

There wouldn't be much opportunity for chance meetings between them, but he knew they would always be close. You couldn't go through as much as they had been through together without becoming life-long friends, even if they couldn't be lovers.

Julia seemed different since Ralph's passing. A softness had come over her where there had been an undertone of bitterness and anger before. She seemed to radiate a new-found joy. To Daniel she looked more beautiful than ever. Now there was more depth and gentleness to her, and a maturity he hadn't seen earlier. Even in his memory of Carmen de la Rosa, standing defiant before the priests of the Inquisition as he lay broken and dying, he had never witnessed such gentle strength. He knew that Julia was finally able to release Carmen's trauma and leave it in the distant past where it belonged.

Daniel half smiled as he watched her strolling past the gravestones hand-in-hand with Frank. Her hair billowed out around her face in the breeze as she earnestly looked up at her friend. What could she be telling him, Daniel wondered? Frank seemed to be mesmerized. Who wouldn't be?

The future looked wide open for Julia and full of potential. Where would she go? Who would she love? For Daniel things were much more predictable. He was young, but he would always have his work as a priest and he was devoted to it. It would fill a lifetime. Still, he envied Frank. He would never have the freedom to take Julia's hand and walk through the first spring wildflowers that had sprung up around the gravestones. And now she was dancing over the fresh-mown lawn, whirling in circles with Frank laughing after her.

Daniel glanced down at the dirt-spattered coffin below him, still and silent. It exuded death. His eyes traveled to the hem of his long black vestment and up to the black prayer book in his hands. Death and more death. All around him people were somber, dressed in black, but overhead the sky arched bright and blue. In the distance birds were singing and blossoms were bursting on the fruit trees, filling the air with heady perfume.

He could hear Julia giggling now and he looked across the cemetery to find her standing atop a large stone cross waving her arms at him. For a moment she looked like a blazing phoenix rising from the ashes of the past.

"Daniel! I love you," she hollered across the tombstone-studded lawn.

Shocked faces of the mourners turned in her direction then back to Father Murphy. He smiled self-consciously, feeling himself blush.

Then with an impulsive grin he raised his arms and shouted, "I love

206

ya too, Julia! Always will." Laughing, he tossed his prayer book onto the coffin.

In one fluid motion he gathered his vestments and took a flying leap over the gaping grave, then sauntered toward his car with an amused smirk on his face. Behind him horrified gasps punctuated his departure.

"I choose to be a priest, but that doesn't mean I have ta join the dead before me time," he spoke aloud to himself as he slipped into his driver's seat. "I'm gonna do it my way — and I'm gonna make some waves!"

He drove slowly past Frank and Julia as they climbed into Frank's beat-up Ford Ranger. Julia turned and grinned at Daniel as he drove by, her amber eyes sparkling with mischief. It was a look he would always remember.

~ END ~

Printed in the United States
by Baker & Taylor Publisher Services